FRANCESCO GUIDICINI

ABOUT THE AUTHOR

NIKKI GEMMELL is the author of several acclaimed novels, including *Shiver*, *Cleave* and *Alice Springs*. She lives in London.

THE
BRIDE
STRIPPED
BARE

A NOVEL

Nikki Gemmell

HARPER **PERENNIAL**

HARPER ● PERENNIAL

First published in 2003 in Great Britain by Fourth Estate as *The Bride Stripped Bare* by Anonymous.

First U.S. edition published in 2004 by Fourth Estate, an imprint of HarperCollins Publishers.

P.S.™ is a trademark of HarperCollins Publishers.

First Harper Perennial edition published 2005.

Designed by Jeffrey Pennington

The Library of Congress has catalogued the hardcover edition as follows:
Gemmell, Nikki.
   The bride stripped bare/Nikki Gemmell.
     p.cm
   ISBN 0-00-716226-X
    1. Marrakech (Morocco)—Fiction. 2. London (England)—Fiction.
3. Married women—Fiction. I. Title.
PR9619.3.G425B75 2004
823'.914—dc21
ISBN-10: 0-06-059188-9 (pbk.)
ISBN-13: 978-0-06-0591885 (pbk.)

05 06 07 08 09 ❖/RRD 10 9 8 7 6 5 4 3

For my husband. For every husband.

Dear Sir,

I am taking the liberty of sending you this manuscript, which I am hoping may interest you.

It was written by my daughter. Twelve months ago, she vanished. Her car was found at the top of a cliff in the south of England, yet her body was never recovered. Despite extensive questioning of several people close to her, the police concluded it was a case of suicide and closed their file. Others speculate that she may have staged her own disappearance. I'm not sure about either scenario and the uncertainty of it all, I must admit has consumed my life.

She was completing a book at the time of her disappearance. It was in her laptop, which the police returned to me. I'm the only person, as far as I know, whom she told about what she'd been working on. It's about a married woman's secret life, and my daughter wished to remain anonymous because she wanted to write with complete candor; she feared she'd only end up censoring herself if her name was attached. She also wanted to protect the people around her, and herself.

I read through her manuscript in the hope of finding a reason for her vanishing, and I felt her life open up before me like a flower. How much I didn't know. How much I didn't want to know. She was a stranger to me in many ways and yet the person closest to me.

My first instinct, I must admit, was to just delete her book and forget about it, but it's been a long time since her going, and even though I've never stopped hoping it will be her on the end of the line when the phone rings, I feel now, that I owe it to help her if I can and find a publisher for her work. I believe it's what she wanted, very much. Her happiness is, ultimately, all I ever wanted for her.

So, here is *The Bride Stripped Bare*. Thank you for your time.

THE BRIDE STRIPPED BARE

1

I have a feeling that inside you somewhere,
there's somebody nobody knows about.

—ALFRED HITCHCOCK AND THORNTON WILDER,
Shadow of a Doubt

Lesson 1

honesty is of the utmost importance

_____

_____

Your husband doesn't know you're writing this. It's quite easy to write it under his nose. Just as easy, perhaps, as sleeping with other people. But no one will ever know who you are, or what you've done, for you've always been seen as the good wife.

Lesson 2

A honeymoon. A foreign land.

There you are, succumbing to the sexual ritual and remembering the day as a seven-year-old when you discovered
water. You'd never been in a swimming pool before; there were
none where you were growing up. You're remembering a summer holiday and a swimming pool with the water inching up
your belly as you stepped forward gingerly and the slow creep
of the cold and the breath collected in the knot of your stomach and your mother always there ahead of you, smiling and
coaxing and holding out her hands and stepping back and
back. Then suddenly, pop, you're floating and the water's
holding your belly and legs like sinews of rope, it's muscular

and balming and silky and the memory's as potent as a first kiss.

As for the first time you fucked, well, you remember the sound, as his fingers readied you between your legs, not much else. Not even a name now.

Lesson 3

<u>making a comfortable bed is a very</u>
<u>important part of household work</u>

In the night air of Marrakech, on your be-
lated honeymoon, the first scrum of morning birds sounds like
fat spitting and crackling in a kitchen. It's still dark but the
birds have taken over from the frogs as crisply as if a conductor's lowered his baton. The call to prayer has pulled you
awake and you can't fall back into sleep, you want to fling the
french doors wide, as wide as they'll go, and inhale the strange
desert dawn. But your husband, Cole, will wake and complain
if you do.

So. You lay your hand on the jut of his hip and breathe
in his sleeping, the sour, sweet smell of it, and smile softly in
the dark. The tip of your nose nuzzles his scent on the back
of his neck.

You've never loved anyone more in your life.

You slip on to the balcony. It's hot, 82 degrees at least. A wondrous child-smile greets a great spill of stars, for the vast orange glow from London's lights means you never see stars at home, scarcely know when there's a full moon. The night flowers exhale their bloom, bougainvillaea and hibiscus and magnolia are still and shadowy in the night. You feel fat with content. Cole calls out, plaintive, and you slip back inside and his arm wings your body and clamps you tight.

Your feet maneuver free of the sheet's smother and dangle off the edge of the bed, as they always do, finding the coolness and the air.

Lesson 4

very few people have many friends; as
the word is generally used, it has no
meaning at all

On the day before you leave for Marrakech
Mrs. Theodora White tells you she has no passion in her life,
for anything. It's such a shock to hear, but she dismisses your
concern with a smile and a flick of her hand. She picks a sliver
of tobacco off her tongue and throws back her head to gulp
the last of her flat white wine. She was born thirty-five
whereas you haven't gained definition yet, haven't hardened
into adulthood. You're also in your thirties but still stamp
through puddles and sing off-key too much, as if tucked inside
you is a little girl who refuses to die.

The only thing I've ever had a passion for was Jesus, Theo
tells you. When I was eleven. It was something to do with the
hips.

She was expelled from your convent school because the Mother Superior decided she had more influence over the students than the nuns did. She has many stories like this. You do not. She's called Diz by the people closest to her. She's always rolling her cigarettes from a battered silver case and this only adds to her charm, as does her air of being constantly in heat. Your friend is lush, ripe, her body a peachy size fourteen. She's one of those women who look like they enjoy an abundance of everything, food, fresh air, sex, laughter, love. When alongside Theo you feel pale, like a leaf left too long in the water, bleached of color and life.

But you don't envy her for you know too much about her. She's your oldest friend in the world, you've loved her since you were thirteen. You're not sure why it's so disturbing to hear she has no passion in her; perhaps it's because your life, in contrast, on the cusp of your honeymoon, seems bathed in love. As you walk home from the café you smile out loud at that thought, you can't help it, you smile widely as you walk down the street.

Lesson 5

<u>it is absolutely necessary to wash the</u>
<u>armpits and hips every day</u>

You've laughed with Theo that your husband always sleeps with his T-shirt and boxer shorts on, even when it's hot. That he doesn't appreciate the sweetness of skin to skin, the softness of it and the smell, the warmth. Just the sight of a man's chest can make you wet. You'd never say an expression like that to him, *makes me wet*. You would to Theo. Cole would be horrified at how much she knows.

You love placing your palm on Cole's chest when you're lying in bed, curving your torso around the crescent of his back, the jigsaw fit of it. You love the smell of him when he hasn't washed, especially the softness under his arms. If he knew, he'd describe it as *unseemly*. Sometimes in bed Cole doesn't allow your hand to stay on his chest, he brusques it away. Sometimes he lets your hand rest there. Sometimes he clamps your hand like it's caught in a trap and when you drag it away he clutches it tight and it becomes a game to disentangle yourself.

But only you're giggling, in the close dark.

Lesson 6

girls can never be too thoughtful

*W*hy are you putting on your socks, you ask.

Because I'm going back to the room, Lovely.

But we've just got here, Donkey. Your swimmers are still wet.

I know, but there's a very important meeting in front of the telly. Are you coming?

No, I'll stay a bit longer.

You feel guilty saying no for Cole needs you a lot and he's loud with his want, it's almost a petulance, like a boy's. But you can feel your skin absorbing this hard Moroccan light like the desert does rain, can feel it uncurling something within you. Here the light bashes you; in England, it licks you.

Cole's skin and eyes recoil from it; his skin is very pale, almost translucent; he's away, inside, a lot. Not only on holidays but in London too. He sequesters himself by habit. At work, until late, or in front of the television, or in the bathroom. He can stay on the toilet for three-quarters of an hour or more, if you sit next to him on the couch he'll make his way to the armchair without even realizing what he's doing, if you put your hand on his groin in bed he'll shrug it away. He sleeps with the curve of his back to you more often than not.

Yet even when he's away he needs you nearby: he's told you that you're his life. You love the ferocity in his need, to be wanted so much. Cole is the only man you're attracted to whom you can talk to without a fear of silence, like an empty highway, right through the middle of the conversation. Or of saying something ridiculous and telling, or of your lip trembling, or of blushing. Your body stays obedient around Cole, you're in control, you can relax. It's one of the reasons why you married him. That you're comfortable with him, that you don't have to act too much, you can be, almost, yourself. No one else is allowed so close.

Lesson 7

dance away with all your might

Y<small>our</small> big toe's kissed, indulgently, when you throw back your arms like a diva on the sunlounger and declare you'll be staying by the pool a little longer. Neither Cole nor yourself has seen anything, yet, of the new city you're in, even though you've been here for four days. Theo would berate you for this but marriage has made you soft, dulled your curiosity. The crush of robed and veiled people at the airport, the mountains of luggage and squealing children and machine-guns on guards were all a little overwhelming, so both Cole and yourself are content to stay wrapped within the hotel for a while. It's like the one in the movie *The Shining*, with wide, deco corridors and a surreally spare lobby and the regret of some long-ago lost decadence. A bastion of French colonialism that's now frequented by wealthy Europeans, but there are not enough of them to plump out its space. There are no Muslims. Perhaps they find it too ridiculous, or unwelcoming, or odd, but there's no one to ask.

You would've sought the answers once, you shone with curiosity once. Now you're almost too languid to care, for you're distracted, deliciously so. You sit on the edge of the pool and dawdle your fingertips in its coolness and remember something from the day-old *Times*, that the urge to think rarely strikes the contented. You smile—so what?—and wave over a pool waiter for another Bellini. How you love them. You've never allowed yourself the luxury of laziness, or four Bellinis in a row before.

A donkey pulls a cart of clippings up a rose-bowered path of the hotel's gardens. A man flicks a whip lazily over the animal's back. It's something of this land at least. You must photograph it.

Lesson 8

<u>it is a wife's duty to make her hus-
band's home happy</u>

Midnight is thick with heat and humming with stillness before the assault of the frogs and the birds and your eyes are shut but you can sense Cole's gaze, can feel his greed and there's a tightness in your throat. Your relationship works delightfully, easily, in so many ways, except for the sex.

But that is not what you married Cole for.

A tongue hits your eye, slug-wet and heavy. Your husband strips away the recalcitrant sheet wound about your legs and nudges, insistently, his knee between your thighs. He must make love on his terms, which isn't often. You usually make love in the mornings to take advantage of his hardness upon waking. Cole's penis often doesn't feel hard enough, as if it's thinking of something else. He doesn't come very often. Both of you usually give up before he has and it's always with relief on your part. You wonder if Cole has a condition that causes him to take so long to come, or if he's undersexed, or just tired. Like you have been, a lot.

As Cole is on top of you on this wide hotel bed you're looking at the numbers of the clock radio by the bed flicking over their minutes and you're thinking of Marilyn Monroe who said *I don't think I do it properly*—you read it in a newspaper once with astonishment and relief: so, someone else, and what a someone else. You're not sure if Cole does it properly, you don't know what properly is. Theo would, for she is a sex therapist with a discreet Knightsbridge office and a Sunday magazine column. You suspect she finds you both innocent and ridiculous and sweet. Cole and you have never done any of that making love twice in a row or knocking over lamps or pulling each other's hair. When you do make love you could describe each other as *tidy*.

The numbers on the clock radio are taking too long to flip over as you lie on the bed, with Cole on top of you. Something has slid away, deep in you. You don't make love often; you've read articles in women's magazines about how frequently most couples do and it always seems such a lot. But no one's completely honest about sex.

Thirteen minutes past midnight. Cole has come. This is rare. He wipes the cum across your breasts and your cheeks and dabs it on your forehead, as if he's blooding you. He's pleased. You're pleased. Perhaps it worked this time. Cole turns on the bedside lamp to assess the soakage on the sheets and any items of clothing; he always does this, he wants it cleaned up as quickly as possible, he hates mess.

You push his face toward you. He's surprised at the boldness, he wants his face back but you hold him firm for you're remembering walking down the aisle and looking ahead to him and your heart swelling with love like an old dried sponge that's been dropped into a bath. When your husband enfolds you in his arms it's a haven, a harbour, to rest from all the toss of the world. It's what you've always wanted, you have to admit, the place of refuge, the cliché.

Lesson 9

the prevention of waste a duty

*B*efore you found Cole you hadn't slept with a man for four years. It's hard, you'd say to Theo, it's really hard. There were the endless birthday nights and New Year's Eves of just you in your bed and no one else. There was the welling up at weddings, the glittery eye-prick, when all the couples would get up to dance. Sometimes it felt like your heart was crazed with cracks like your grandmother's old saucers. Sometimes the sight of a Saturday afternoon couple laughing in a park would splinter it completely. Young couples who'd been together for many years were intriguing, hateful, remote. What was their secret? You'd reached the stage where you couldn't imagine ever being in a loving partnership.

Theo had warned you that any person who lives by themselves for more than three years becomes strange and selfish and has to be hauled back into the world. She said she had to intervene. You told her no, you were beyond help, you'd convinced yourself of this. All your life people had been leaving: you were a child of divorced parents and you never grew up with the expectation that someone would look after you, and stay.

But then Cole McCain.

An old acquaintance from university, a friend, just that. One summer you were house-sitting in Edinburgh during the festival and he asked if he could come to stay; there were some shows he wanted to catch. You remember marching him to his room, a little girl's, with its narrow bed and pink patchwork quilt. You remember his dubious look.

I think you better sleep in the big bed with me, you said.

It was meant to be two friends bunking down for the sake of convenience. You both had your pajamas on, you made sure of that. But then his sudden fingers on your skin were like a trickle of water on a sweltering summer's day. A strangeness shot through you, you turned to him, kissed. Cole stripped off his pajamas, quick, and then yours were off too and something took over you, you were gone. Within a week you were both rolling up in the sheets and falling off the bed in a giggly cocoon. Within two years you were married.

I've known for years, you wally, said Theo in gleeful hindsight, it was always so obvious.

I never saw it.

It had taken you a long time to wake up to some sense. You used to sleep with men you were uncomfortable with in an attempt to make yourself comfortable with them; you married the one you forget yourself with.

But there was a moment of invisibility when you tried on the wedding dress, as if you were disappearing into that swathe of ivory and tulle, being wiped away. It was only fleeting and it was worth it, of course, not to have the prickle behind the eyes of those laughing Saturday afternoon couples again, the heart-crack.

Lesson 10

Men you have slept with. What you remember the most:

The one who loved women.

The one who never took off his socks.

The one whose hands were so big they seemed to be in
three places at once.

The one whose touch hummed, who seemed to know
exactly what he was doing and stood out because of that.
He seemed only to derive pleasure from the experience if
you were, whereas none of the others seemed too fussed. He
asked what your fantasies were but you didn't have the courage
to speak out. Back then, you'd never have the courage for
that.

22

The one who sent you a polaroid of his very big cock.*
But size means little to you, you don't know why they go on
about it. You much prefer a comfortable fit than a penis that's
too big; you don't want to feel you're being split apart.

The one who'd say *take me* as he came and groaned like
he was doing a big shit.

The one who tickled you behind your knees and licked
you on the face, who forced you to swallow his cum and
rubbed it through your hair; who was aroused by all the things
you didn't like.

The one who said yes, when you asked him to marry you,
half joking, half not, on a February the twenty-ninth. You're
embarrassed you had to ask Cole McCain. You wish he'd never
mention it, but he does, in a teasing way, a lot.

---

*You're more than happy to write the word *cock*; saying it aloud, how-
ever, is another matter. It even feels a little odd to say *vagina* but you're
not sure what else to use. You hate *pussy*, you don't know any woman
who says it, and as for *cunt*, you always think it's used by men who don't
like women very much. You want some words that women have colonized
for themselves; maybe they exist but you haven't heard them yet. You
can't say *down there* for the rest of your life.

Lesson 11

<u>a sacred and delicate reticence should always enwrap the pure and modest woman</u>

*E*arly morning.

A bird flaps into the room and you wake, panicked at the flittering above your head and run to the bathroom and slam the door, begging Cole to do something, quick. The bird's swiftly gone. It hasn't crashed wildly into mirrors or windows. You couldn't bear that—you witnessed it once as a child, the droppings out of fright, the too-bright blood, the crazed thump, the shrill eye.

But now there's just quiet hovering in the room. You step into it from the bathroom and kiss Cole on the tip of his nose. He envelops you in his arms with a great calm of ownership and laughs: he likes you vulnerable. And to teach you, to introduce you to new things. You didn't look closely at a penis until you were married, didn't know what a circumcised one looked like. You wonder, now, how you could've had the partners you've had and never really looked. You always wanted the lights off quick because you never liked your body enough, and dived under the sheets, and felt it was rude to study a man's anatomy too intently: you favored eye contact and touch. Cole forced you to look, right at the start, he taught you to get close. He likes to direct your life, to guide it.

You let him think he is.

Lesson 12

<u>it is our greatest happiness to be</u>
<u>unselfish</u>

Cole fell asleep inside you once. He laughs at the memory, finds it erotic and silly and comforting. The morning after, to soothe your indignation, he'd said that falling asleep inside a woman was a sign of true love.

What? Shaking your head as if rattling out a fly.

It means that the man's truly comfortable with the woman, so comfortable that he can fall asleep in the process of making love to her. I could never do that to anyone else. Think yourself honored, Lovely.

Hmm, you'd replied.

You love Cole in a way you haven't loved before. Calmly. It glows like a candle rather than glitters. You love him even when he falls asleep in the process of making love to you. You'd never loved calmly before, in your twenties. That was the time of greedy love, full of exhilaration and terror, and when you said *I love you* you always felt stripped; there was no sense, ever, of love as a rescue. Sometimes, now, you wonder what happened to the intensity of your youth, when everything seemed so vivid and desperate and bright. Sometimes you imagine a varnisher's hand whipping over the quietness of your life now and flooding it with brightness, combusting it, in a way, with light.

But Cole. When he enfolds you in his arm you feel his love running as quiet and strong and deep as an underground river right through you. He stills your agitation in the way a visit to Choral Evensong does, or a long swim after work. The bond between you seems so clear-headed: the marriage is not perfect, by any means, but you're old enough now to know you cannot demand perfection from the gift of love. It's a lot more than most people have. Like Theo.

Your dear, restless, vivid-hearted friend. Sometimes you feel a sharp envy at the sensuality of her home, all candles and wood and stone, her fluid working hours, weekly massages, Kelly bags. But you remind yourself that she isn't happy and probably never will be and it's a comfort, that. For no matter how much Theo achieves and acquires and out-dazzles everyone else, she never seems content. She's taught you that people who shine more lavishly than everyone else seem to be penalized by discontent, as if they're being punished for craving a brighter life. I've been knocked down so many times I can't remember the number plates, she said once.

Many people are afraid of Theo but you've never been, perhaps that's why you're so close. All the noise of her personality is a mask and when it slips off, on the rare occasion, the vulnerability riddled through her is always a shock.

Lesson 13

it cannot be rational enjoyment to go
where you would not like to have your
truest and best friend go with you

*H*old my hand, Cole says as he steers you
through the twilight crush of Marrakech. Neither of you knows
the pedestrian etiquette of this city; the cars are coming in all
directions, the dusky streets teem like rush hour in New York
but everything's faster, cheekier, more reckless; exhilarating,
you think. Mopeds and tourist coaches and donkeys and carts
stop and start and weave and cut each other off without, it
seems, any rules and the scrum of people funnels you into the
great sprawling square at the city's heart, Djemma El Fna, and
you lift your head to the low ochre-colored buildings around
you and break from Cole's grasp and swirl, gulping the sights,
for you feel as if all of life's in this place. There are snake-

charmers with arms draped by writhing snake necklaces, wizened storytellers ringed by attentive men, water sellers with belts of brass cups like ropes of ammunition, veiled women offering fortunes, jewellery, hennaed hands. It's a movie set of the glorious, the bizarre, the deeply kitsch.

Diz would love all this, you laugh.

Thank God you didn't bring her.

You'd almost invited her on the spot when she said she was so low. You wanted her to join you just for a couple of days, as a treat: it's her birthday in three days, June the first. But you knew you'd have to check with Cole first and he wouldn't stand for it, of course.

She's weird, he says of her.

You say that about all my friends.

She's weirder than the rest.

You can't argue with that. Theo takes the train to Paris just for a haircut. Has a tattoo of a gardenia below her pubic line. Can't poach an egg. Never watches television. Gets her favorite flowers delivered to herself every Monday and Friday: iceberg roses, November lilies, exquisite gardenia knots. Is married to a man called Tomas, twenty-four years her senior, whom she's rarely made love to. She has a condition.

What, you'd asked, when she first told you.

Vaginismus. It sounds vile, doesn't it? Like something you'd pick up in Amsterdam. It means that when anyone tries to fuck me the muscles around my vagina go into spasms. It's excruciatingly painful.

Theo, darling Theo, of all people. You wrapped her in a hug, your face crumpled, you began to cry.

Hey, it's OK, she laughed, it's OK. It's actually been rather fun.

And she leant back and smiled her trademark grin, one side up, one side down. Took out her little silver case. Lit a cigarette. Said that she'd decided to investigate the whole situation, a woman's pleasure, and it was so deliciously consuming that it eventually slipped into being a job. Said that most women never climaxed from vaginal penetration: all the fun was in the clit. You'd blushed back then, at hearing the bluntness of that word, there were some things you couldn't help.

I can't tell you how many clients get absolutely no pleasure whatsoever out of bog-standard penetration, she said, punctuating her words with savage little taps that made the cutlery jump. We just don't know how to please ourselves enough. We'll never learn. We're still too intent on the man's pleasure at the expense of our own.

You weren't entirely comfortable with this talk, it was a little close to the bone. You wanted to know more of her condition, for it was a strange relief to hear that your arrestingly sensual friend also had stumbling blocks over sex: so, Theo was human, too.

Did you get some help, for the vagi, vagis—

Mm, I did. It involved a horrible thing called a dilator.

Did it work?

Well, yes, but when I finally had the sex I'd been waiting

for it was such a let-down. It's so dull compared with everything else. Why didn't anyone tell me this?

Theo's wonderful laugh curdled from deep in her belly but there was no joy in her eyes. Her marriage to Tomas was so odd, you couldn't figure it out. He had other relationships with men as well as women and she had relationships with women as well as men, that was their life. And yet they stayed together. *I don't have any passion in my life, for anything.* Not for her husband, whom she says she's too clever to love. Nor for London, the city of fractious energy you both fled to as teenagers from the same boarding school, almost twenty years ago. Nor for her job, for she says she's been doing it so long that the stories are now all the same, there aren't many new plots in people's lives and she's found, lately, she's switching off.

You suspect you attract extreme people like her because you're so stable, as is Cole. She described the two of you once as eerily content and for some this means unforgivably beige but for others you're an anchor, always there if needed, even on Sunday evenings, and birthdays, and Christmas Day.

Theo and you have shared your lives since the age of thirteen; swapping Arabian stud magazines for the pictures of the horses, camping overnight for tickets to Duran Duran, devouring books in tandem, from *Little House on the Prairie* to *The Thorn Birds* and *Story of* O. Having your first cigarette together and the last shower you've ever shared with a girl. Standing to the left of each other at wedding altars, knowing you'll be godmothers to each other's children.

You met in the same class at a minor boarding school in Hampshire, a place where mediocrity was encouraged. You were not meant to be clever, since being clever did not make you a good wife. If you excelled at anything it was seen as a mild perversion but Theo was stunningly oblivious to that. Not many people liked her at first. She came to the class in the middle of term. She'd developed earlier than the other girls and had foreign parents, New Zealanders, who'd made their money only recently, and not nearly enough. But through force of personality she turned her fortune round and was made a prefect, as were you.

Don't get too excited, she told you, practically *everyone's* been made one. They've only done it because they forgot to educate us—it's something to put on our CVs.

She was expelled for writing to the Pope, explaining to him why the rhythm method of contraception, for a lot of girls, just didn't work. (She'd learnt this lesson from her older sister, who'd had an abortion in secret.) Her mistake was to sign the letter with the name of a blond classmate who was going to be a model when she grew up and was promised a car, by her father, if she stopped biting her nails. And was extremely accomplished at looking down on you both. The scandal made Theo a heroine-in-exile but she always remained supremely faithful to you, the lady-in-waiting who'd fallen in love with her first.

Here, in Marrakech, you just wish your friend were as happy as you for you want others to be joyous, to bring them joy, you get such a deep satisfaction from that. You'd love to have Theo here, to cheer her up; it'd be someone to see the sights with while Cole was off by himself. You're always doing small kindnesses; your grandmother told you never to suppress a kind thought and you always try not to. You snap a shot of a snake man in the square and he rushes toward you, hustling for coins and waving his snakes and you squeal away from him, pulling Cole with you. You must tell her.

Lesson 14

Dinner's dared in the square on rough wooden benches at a smoky stall. Cole and you pick at the couscous but ignore the gnarled-looking meat on kebabs and gritty salad, and have your photo taken as proof of your courage. Cole's tetchy and irritable and wants to get back to the too-quiet hotel but you feel like you're at the center of a vast meeting place of African tribes from the south and Arabs from the north and Berber villagers from the mountains and you hold your head high and drink in the smells and heat and smoke. All these wondrous people! You look across at your husband and stroke his arm, his thin, sensual wrist, and there's a stirring of desire: you want him, really want him, in that way, in this crowded place. You do nothing but hold your lips to his skin in the clearing behind his ear and breathe in. It's usually enough, some small gesture like this, just to touch him, to inhale him, to remind you of what you've got.

But here, now, something dormant within you is stretching awake, is arching its back. You think of the hotel room and the expanse of the bed. For just a fleeting moment you imagine yourself naked with your legs wide and several anonymous, assessing men and their hands running over you. You imagine being filmed, being bought.

You smile at Cole.

What are you thinking, he asks.

Nothing, you murmur.

Lesson 15

<u>there are few wives who do not</u>
<u>heartily desire a child</u>

A s you laze on your deckchairs a heavily pregnant woman strides to the swimming pool like a galleon in full sail, robust and proud and complete. You'll be trying for a baby soon, once the first year of marriage is done.

Let's just enjoy ourselves for a while, Cole has said.

But thank goodness a pregnancy is secure in the plans. Man, house, child: such happiness is obscene in one person, isn't it? There's such an audacity in the joy you now feel. How could anyone bear you? You glance across at Cole: he looked too young for so long, not fully formed, but now, in his late thirties, when a lot of his peers are losing hair and gaining weight, it's all starting to work. He'd been in a state of arrested adolescence but now he's filled out and he's handsome, at last.

He has the potential to age into magnificence and you're only just seeing it.

Shouldn't it be wearing off, this fullness in your heart fit to burst? When's it meant to wilt? You throw down your *Vogue* and place your body on Cole's, belly to belly, and breathe in his skin like a mother does with a child. Will that scent ever sour for you? You can't imagine how. He pushes you off, mock grumpy, and slaps you on the bum. You shriek and settle again on your lounger. A young waiter walks by. You narrow your eyes like a cat and laze your arms over your head and tell Cole that if you're not treated properly it's the waiter you'll be marrying next.

Yeah, and all he'll have to do to get rid of you is say I divorce thee three times. I wish it were that easy for me.

You laugh; you're filled up with joy, it's all bubbling out. The pregnant woman steps out of the pool. People have begun asking when Cole and you are going to start a family and your husband always replies that he'll have a child when he considers himself grown-up, and God knows when that will be. You tell them soon.

All women must want children eventually, you're sure, that furious need is deep in their bones, you don't quite believe any woman who says she doesn't. The urge has begun to harangue you as your thirties march on, it's an animal instinct grown bold. Your heart will now tighten whenever you see the imprint of a friend in her child's face. It's something that's in danger of overtaking your life, the want.

Lesson 16

<u>all nature is lovely and worthy of our
reverent study</u>

*O*n a day trip to the Atlas Mountains you hold your head out the car window, to the sky, the scent of eucalyptus on the baked breeze. Cole reads the *Herald Tribune* and dozes and snaps awake.

He works extremely hard as a picture restorer, specializing in paintings from the fifteenth to the nineteenth centuries. He now travels the globe, preparing condition reports for paintings to be sold and working on site, for since September eleventh the insurance premiums have skyrocketed and it's often cheaper to fly the restorer to the job. Cole's days are long but the rewards are great—you no longer have to work. Indolence is something you've always wanted to try and this is your second month of doing nothing. Cole encouraged you to quit your job as a lecturer in journalism at City University; he'd bulldozed your trepidation with his enthusiasm. Redundancies were on offer and the sum cleared the mortgage for you both. None of your colleagues wanted you to go; you were a stabilising presence in a temperamental faculty, you kept your head down, worked hard. But you'd been worn thin by years of teaching, the relentless routine of work eat sleep and little else, it had become like a net dragging you down. Theo said you'd been so noble, so selfless as a teacher that it was bound to take its toll. You didn't tell her it felt cowardly that you'd never actually left university and entered the real world; you just teased that she was a teacher also and every bit as noble as yourself.

God no, I do my job purely for me and no one else. It's utterly selfish what I get from it.

And what, my dear, is that?

This secret thrill, she grinned, as my clients tell me all their deepest, darkest thoughts.

Your job had stopped being gratifying in any way and you delight in the strange feeling of satisfaction from doing this new wifely life well. You weren't expecting your days to be swallowed by so many mundanities but you're oddly enjoying, for the moment, cooking fiddly Sunday meals on week nights and painting the kitchen and sorting through clothes. The days gallop by even though you know that boredom and a loss of esteem could one day yap at your heels. But not now, not yet.

You have little left in the way of savings but Cole pays you an allowance of eight hundred pounds a month. It's meant a subtle change: he now has a licence to expect darned socks and home-made puddings, to comment a touch too often on your rounded stomach or occasional spots. But his small cruelties are a small price to pay for the luxury of resting. He's giving you something you've never had before: a chance to recuperate and to work out what you want to do with the rest of your life. You've been so tight and controlled for so long, always on time and everything just so. During the first month of unemployment you gulped sleep and suspect it's years of exhaustion catching up on you, all the trying to please, the never being able to say no. Anyway, Cole's teasing is done in a silly, childlike way and you never mind very much.

On this day trip to the Atlas Mountains he's here under protest, he wants to go back. He hates activity and the outdoors of any sort, he pretends to be so fusty and curmudgeonly, at such a young age, but you find it adorable, he makes you laugh so much. And there's an intriguing flip side to his crustiness, the little boy who watches *Star Trek* and buys Coco Pops. You love the kid in the T-shirt under the Italian suits; you're the only one, you suspect, who knows anything of it.

On the narrow dirt road the car winds and slows and you want to jump out and whip off your shoes and feel the ochre as soft as talcum powder claiming your feet. You know deep in your bones this type of land, for you visited places not dissimilar, with your mother, when you were young. The Sahara is just over the mountains, the desert of smoking sand and tall skies.

It's a desert the color of wheat, says Muli, the driver and guide.

How lovely, and you clap your heavily hennaed hands. The sight of them entrances you. You must take us, Muli, you say.

Cole glances across.

Next time.

You smile and lick your husband under the ear, like a puppy, he's so funny, it's all a game, and you're filled like a glass with love for him, to the brim.

Lesson 17

<u>the duty of girls is to be neat and tidy</u>

Cole more often than not dislikes fingers touching his bare skin, he'll flinch at contact without warning. Your fingertips are always cold: in winter when you want to touch him you'll warm your fingers beforehand on the hot-water bottle, he insists.

Cole's life is very neat. He re-irons his shirts after the cleaning lady has, shines his shoes every Sunday night, leaves for work promptly at eight fifteen, jumps to the bathroom soon after sex to mop up the spillage.

There are some things you suspect Cole prefers to making love. Like his head being scratched so hard that flakes of skin gather under your nails, which you detest. And having the skin of his back stroked with a comb like a soft rake through soil, reaping goose bumps. And resting his head on the saddle of your back as you lie on your stomach in a summer park.

And going down on him. This, only this, is guaranteed to make him come. Sometimes you go down on him just to get it all over with quickly. Cole pushes your head on to him as far as he can and then a little further, and when you bob up for air he measures with his thumb and finger how far you've gone and duly you marvel, the good wife, and bob down again. You often gag, or have to break the rhythm to come up for air, your jaw always aches, it goes on too long. You hate the taste of sperm, you recoil from it, like a tongue on cold metal in winter.

Go home and give him one, Theo said once, after a cinema night. The poor thing, it's been so long.

God no, please, not that.

If you give them blow jobs they love you for life.

But it's such a *chore*.

I see it as a challenge.

You took Theo's advice: Cole told you, when it was done, that he couldn't wait for the next movie night with your mate.

Calm down, you laughed, and rolled over and went to sleep.

It wasn't always like this. In the early days you'd make love almost every single night. Cole would sing and dance around in his underwear and be completely stupid before he dived into bed. Have you laughing so much that it hurt. You'd always be completely naked down to the removal of watches, there was a gentle courtesy to that. You'd have sex, daringly for you both, in sleeper carriages from London to Cornwall, as giggly as teenagers as you tried to be quiet for the children next door. Or in your teenage bed that your mother has kept, with Cole's hand clamped on your mouth to keep you quiet. You cried tears of happiness and he kissed them up, his palms muffing your cheeks and you still have, pocketed in your memory, the tenderness in his touch.

But those moments, now, seem like scenes from a movie; not quite real. The woman in them is removed, someone else. This is real, now: you've shut down, there are other things you'd rather do. It's such a bother removing all your clothes and finding time to do it and making sure you smell sweet and clean. It never seems to be the best time, for both of you at once, there's always something that's not quite right. Either you're not in the mood or Cole isn't and it's become easy to make an excuse. You both, it seems, would prefer to be reading newspapers, or watching TV, or sleeping. Most of all that.

Cole doesn't protest too much. The marriage is about something else. He's kind, is always doing astonishingly kind things, it's as if he's binding you to him with kindness. There are subscriptions to favorite, frivolous magazines, unexpected cups of tea, frog-marching you to bed when you're overtired, the gift of a new book that he's wedged somewhere in the bookshelf and says you must find. All these little gestures force you into kindness too, kindness begets kindness, the marriage is almost a competition of kindness. So there's scratching his head so hard that flakes of skin gather under your nails, and acquiescence in bed, and blow jobs. These small kindnesses buy Cole time alone, away from you, away from the world, within his halo of light in front of the television or in the bathroom or studio until late. You don't mind the alone either, you need it too, to breathe again, to uncurl.

It's a strange beast, your marriage, it's irrational, but it works. It's traditional, and how judgmental your mother is of that. She was divorced young and raised you by herself until you were sent to boarding school. She instilled in you that you should never rely on a man; you had to be financially independent, you mustn't succumb. But it's a relief, to be honest, this surrendering of the feminist wariness. It feels naughty and delicious and indulgent, like wearing a bit of fur.

Lesson 18

sound sleep is a condition essential to
good health

---

*O*ne A.M. You're reading the first Harry Potter. It's Cole's, you found it among the rest of his holiday books, weighty tomes on history and art. You're in the armchair by the French doors to the balcony, a leg dangling over the arm.

A spider of sweat slips down your torso. You'd love to feel a storm breaking the back of the heat, to hear it rumbling in the floorboards and smell it in the lightning. You look across at Cole, sleeping on the sheet with his shoes still on. You slip them off like a mother with a toddler and roll him over to remove his shirt; he's stirring, reaching for you, scrabbling at your skirt. Sssh, you tell him, and you hold your lips to the dip in the back of his neck. You don't want him properly waking, don't want anything to start. For you've begun menstru-ating and the blood's leaking out of you, hot, and you know he'd be appalled by this. He doesn't like blood.

Cole usually sleeps soundly, the sleep of a man content. He's not a snorer, you could never marry him if he were. How could you secure a decent night's sleep with a man who snores? Cole laughed when you told him this on your wedding night; it's the only reason why I married you, you said. Cole responded that if he *did* snore he'd borrow one of your bras and put tennis balls in it and wear it back to front, to stop him from sleeping on his back, that's how much he loved you.

One thing you could never tell your husband is that his coming takes too long. And that his penis seems bent, and of-ten goes soft in you, as if it's thinking of something else. And that the reason he got blow jobs all the time, when the rela-tionship was young, was to butter him up. And to make him think you were someone else.

Lesson 19

good habits are best learnt in youth

You sit by the concierge desk in the vast almost empty lobby while Cole changes some cash. A man passes, he wears the sun in his face, he's a boy really, a decade or so younger than you and he smiles right into your eyes and you feel something you haven't for years: it's to do with university parties with bathtubs of alcohol and the smell of hamburgers on fingers and beer in a kiss. You should have been disgusted by all that but you weren't. You'd be wet so quick; to get their clothes off, to have their weight upon you, to be rammed against a wall with your leg curled up.

You're singing inside as you saunter back with Cole to your room of fresh roses. Every second day new roses await you, they're never allowed to wilt in the heat. Inside, you kiss your husband fully on the mouth, surprising yourself as much as him with the ferocity of it. You taste him, drink him, and you so rarely do that. He kisses you back in his way, as if inside your mouth is the most exquisite, expensive morsel imaginable. You don't like him kissing you on the lips very much; often you secretly wipe away the track that's left by his mouth.

The last time Cole and you had made love, before this holiday, was your wedding night. The vintage Bugatti you'd borrowed wouldn't start and all Cole's distant relatives had to be met and Theo got too drunk. Cole and you had ended up giddy and sweaty back at your hotel room, ravenous, with just a Mars Bar from the mini bar to share between you. Still, there was a new sweetness to making love, even though it was soaked in a sudden tiredness and a little clumsy, and you didn't get far: almost an afterthought to the end of a long day. It didn't matter that the sex on that night wasn't the best you'd ever had, for you'd been together for so long before that.

The honeymoon had been delayed because Cole was always accepting another commission and getting tied up. He finally found a window of escape four months after you'd tied the knot. You didn't complain, you appreciate his attachment to his job, it's so solid, so dependable: he'll never let you down.

He's never given you an orgasm. He assumes he has. You're a good actress—a lot of women are, you suspect. You know what you're supposed to do, the sounds you make and the arching of the back and the clenched face: it's in a thousand movies to mimic, it's everywhere but your own life. You've never had an orgasm by yourself or with any man that you've slept with. You've lied to every one of them that you have, that it's worked. You're curious about them but not curious enough. It's like a language you don't speak; you know you should make an attempt at it but you can get by perfectly happily without it, it's not going to impede your life. You're in your mid-thirties and have never even looked down there, at yourself. Cole could tell you about it if you were curious enough, but the intimacies of your own body are for someone else, you feel, not yourself.

Lesson 20

to be delicate is considered by some
ignorant people as an enviable distinc-
tion

*G*in and tonics by the pool.

Cole reads aloud an extract from the historical section of the *Herald Tribune*. A woman in New Jersey in 1925, a mother of eight, was inspired by *Ali Baba and the Forty Thieves* to heat a cauldron of olive oil and pour it over her sleeping husband.

Oil, Lovely, can you believe it, *oil*.

But you're hardly listening for you're thinking of the man in the lobby and your very first fuck, with the TV show *The Young Ones* flicking mute in the background and how tight and dry and uncomfortable it had been. You're thinking of the boy's distasteful triumph afterward, with his mates, and the TV turned up too loud. You're thinking of Theo—but it all sounds so . . . squalid—as she dragged on her cigarette with uncommon ferocity. How strange you can't recall her own account of her loss of virginity. It's something you can't remember talking about, in fact, with any of your girlfriends. Were a lot of the experiences as disappointing as yours, is that why they're never discussed; do you all want to move on? You're remembering that Theo had put copper lipstick in her hair back then to highlight the colour because she'd read it in a magazine but you're not remembering, for the life of you, the boy's name.

You're thinking of Sean, the student Theo and you shared a flat with. He was still hopelessly, consumingly in love with an older woman who'd broken his heart and he never made an effort to become a part of the household; his days were spent moping, alone. One day he disappeared. The police came to your front door a week later and told you that he'd taken a train to Scotland and hitched to a remote beach where his lover had her holiday cottage and he'd swum out to sea and had never swum back. You were haunted by that for years afterward, the wild, jagged love that Sean had, and of the outside leaking into him, the water swelling his flesh and lapping at his bones. He was brave in a way, to do that, you'd thought that for so long. Now, you just wish he'd grown up and known other women, that he'd journeyed to a point in his life where he could look back and laugh.

Lesson 21

exercise is quite as requisite for girls
as it is for lions and tigers

Muli takes you to Yves St. Laurent's public garden, sheltered and cool within high walls. The noise of Marrakech falls away as you enter. This would be Theo's kind of place. It's spiky and seductive with cacti and palms and splashes of blue paint and bougainvillaea-pink cascading over walls. You take a photo for her. You'll tuck it in an envelope, with some rose petals from the room.

You escape the press of the heat in the winding coolness of the market alleyways. You love the souks, the instrument shop that could have existed several hundred years ago next to a shop selling live iguanas next to one crammed with Sylvester Stallone T-shirts. Love the donkeys in the alleys and skinny cats and red Coca-Cola signs in Arabic, the attacking light, the dust heavy on your skin and clotting your hair, the mountains rimming the city, the talking dark, the crickets and dogs and frogs. There's the call to prayers and Muli excuses himself for ten minutes. You love the pervasiveness of religion in this place, how the chant wakes you in darkness and plots your day. Cole admires the colors of the city, the vaulting blue of the sky and rich ochres and pinks but he can't bear the dust and the cram and the heat, he's very loud about all that, he's not enjoying being dragged around.

Your confidence is softly leaking as a wife. You'd never tell him. That you sometimes feel as if all the men through your life, the lovers, colleagues, bosses, with their clamor and demand, have been rubbing you out.

Cole's in another meeting. He's resorted to watching Pokémon cartoons in French, a language he doesn't understand, for the English stations carry just rolling news and the stories aren't changing enough. There are also local news broadcasts with items that run for twenty minutes and seem to be made up entirely of long shots of the King on parade or men in suits on low chairs. The news anchor's young, with the most beautiful eyes, it's as if they have kohl round them. You wonder what he'd be like as a lover, if he'd be *different*. You've heard that Muslim women are shaved and all at once you feel a soft tugging between your legs, thinking of that; and of being robed, for your husband's eyes only. Muli told you both that no one's ever laid eyes on the Queen, she's not seen in public, is hidden.

I like that, Cole had laughed.

And was playfully hit.

Later, over gin and tonics in the piano bar Cole holds his cheek to yours and whispers that he wants to lock you up and never allow you out and he wants another wife as well as you, whom you'll have to sleep with, while he's watching, and your hands cup his face: You are so predictable, McCain, you chuckle and kiss him gently on each cheek and it stirs something in you, memories of Edinburgh and rolling off a bed and making love with a hand clamped across your mouth.

Lesson 22

<u>making a noise is of itself healthy,</u>
<u>when no one is inconvenienced or</u>
<u>annoyed by it</u>

*S*ometimes you wonder if your husband really *likes* women. He speaks dismissively of your girlfriends and female colleagues, doesn't want a wife who's pushy or loud, gets annoyed if you talk to your girlfriends too boomingly on the phone and winces if you shriek. He doesn't like excesses in women of any kind. He niggles when you don't dry yourself thoroughly after the bath, says it's so moist down there you must be growing a jungle. His genitals smell unoffensive, milder than your own.

Cole's parents are very together, very solidly, defensively middle class. They don't think you'll look after their son well enough. His mother communicates all her vigor through her cooking and is horrified you've only recently learnt how to do a roast. She sends correspondence, persistently, to Mr and Mrs C. McCain despite you telling her you haven't changed your name.

Cole thinks your family is eccentric. It used to be delightfully, exotically so, until he got to know them. Your great-great-grandfather made his fortune importing tea from India and your father's cousin frittered away the remains of the family wealth on drinking and drugs. Your father was from the poor side of the family and was meant to work but never got around to it. He was charming and roguish, all blond hair and cheekbones in his youth, until drink sapped his looks. You adored him because you never saw him enough. He survived by periodically cashing in shares of the family business until he died, when you were nineteen, of drunkenness and poverty and a spineless life.

It broke your heart. Seeing him during your teenage years seemed to consist, almost entirely, of a series of journeys to and from school. He'd pick you up in his old black Mercedes that looked like a relic from some totalitarian regime, and drive and drive, picking the smallest, most winding country lanes to get you to London. It was only in the car that you ever seemed to talk, because his girlfriend, Karen, always made it difficult when you were in their flat; butting into your time and crying over God knows what. Your father's affection was reserved for the road or the odd moments when Karen was out of the room, when he'd lean across and whisper *I love you* as if it was a secret between you. His voice, now, is what you remember most.

Your parents' marriage lasted four months. Your mother left its volatility two weeks after you were conceived, left it to hunt for fossils. She'd studied palaeontology at university but had halted the career to be the wife. Your father refused to live anywhere but London even though your mother was an asthmatic who dreamt of a light that would sing in her lungs. Work provided that, and so as a child you lived in a succession of places that were singed by the sky until the courts intervened, at your father's orders (the only thing he ever managed to do in his life, snapped your mother, more than once) and you were sent back to England, the land of soft days, and, when you grew up, orgasmless fucks.

People who know nothing of your family find it fascinating and charming and extreme but Cole now knows the truth, that little of that extremity has rubbed off on you; it's only reinforced your own caution. You've had to be sensible, had to make a living amid all the chaos.

Cole says your mother is bruised by bitterness, that she's menopausal and mad and he fears you'll turn into her. He doesn't enjoy visiting her cottage on the north Yorkshire coast, an area that's rich in the fossils of marine reptiles and fish. It's wilfully remote and she's hardly ever home because she's always off on a dig. He doesn't enjoy the way she absently picks up his toothbrush to scrub at a piece of sandstone she's working on (or perhaps deliberately, but you could never tell Cole that) and clutters her house with old bones and rocks. Cole finds her selfish and sloppy: she's the type of person who washes up in lukewarm water, he said once, and you laughed at the time but didn't forget.

You've tried hard to be nestled within Cole's family, to be the good wife, but they never trust you enough. Cole doesn't understand that a stable family's one of the most desirable things of all when you've come from a fractured childhood, doesn't understand the terrible, Grand Canyon loneliness you feel within his. But you have each other, a sure path, a certainty. Home fills his heart when Cole's on the road, he just longs for the vivid tranquillity of your flat. It's his sanctuary from all the anxiety of the world: paintings too traumatized to repair and canny fakes and deadlines impossible to meet. You're careful not to butt anything too unsettling into his stressful life for you're so lucky, you know that. Your husband's a modern man who's generous and thoughtful, who cooks and cleans; who's devoted, Theo says, you're one of the few couples who are truly happy. And she should know. She's seen a lot of couples. When the women bring their men for coaching sessions to her studio she literally gets into the bed with them both, armed with a pair of latex gloves and a vibrator.

I'd love to have a session with you guys, she's said, as if she wants to bottle the secrets of why your relationship works.

God no, you'd replied, laughing, appalled. You've never been able to shit in a public loo if another woman was in the room, let alone have sex. When you shared a shower with Theo, at the age of thirteen, it was so excruciating that you vowed you'd never get yourself into such a situation again. You could strip off at a doctor's surgery or in a public gym, where you were utterly anonymous, but it was another matter entirely with someone you knew, and so well.

No one, though, has any idea of the churn of a secret life. Your desire to crash catastrophe into your world is like a tugging at your skirt. But only sometimes, and then it's gone. With the offer of a bath, or a cup of tea, or the dishes done.

Lesson 23

You have a book given to you by your grandfather that's a delicious catalog of unseemly thoughts:

That a wife should take another man if her husband is disappointing in the sack.

That a woman's badness is better than a man's goodness.

That women are more valiant than men.

That Adam was more sinful than Eve.

It was written anonymously, in 1603. It's scarcely bigger
than the palm of your hand. The paper is made of rag, not
wood pulp, and the pages crackle with brittleness as they're
turned. You love that sound, it's like the first lickings of a
flame taking hold. The book is titled *A Treatise proveinge by
sundrie reasons a Woemans worth* and its words were contained

once by two little locks that at some point have been snapped off. It smells of confinement and secret things.

You imagine a chaste and good wife writing secretly, gleefully, late at night and in the long hours of the afternoon. A beautiful, decorative border of red and black ink hems each page. It's a fascinating, disobedient labor of love. You wear cotton gloves to open it. You'll never sell it.

It's been in the family for generations. A rumor persists that the author's skeleton was found in some cupboard under a staircase, that she'd been locked into it after her husband discovered her book. Your father told you stories of her scrabbling at a door and crying out and of her despairing nail marks gouged into the wood, but you suspect the reality is much more prosaic: that your great-grandfather acquired the book at auction, as a curiosity, and it may even have been written by a man, as an enigmatic joke.

Cole calls it The Heirloom, or alternatively, The Scary Book. He teases that he'll toss it in the bin if you're naughty, or lock you in the cupboard and never let you out. You love all this banter between you; he makes you laugh so much. You never see any irony in it. He calls the bits and pieces of your father's furniture dotted about the flat The Ruins. And you, affectionately, The Old Boot. It never fails to get a rise out of you; Cole loves seeing that.

Lesson 24

<u>the chief causes of the weak health of women are silence, stillness and stays; therefore learn to sing and dance, and never wear tight stays</u>

*T*he hanging sky. The air smelling of the sea. You don't even need an umbrella as you lie on a sun lounger next to the pool. The breeze blowing in from the desert plays havoc with your *Herald Tribune* and you give up and watch the people around you, you're more interested in the women's bodies than the men's, all women are, Theo has said and she's right. You remember exactly her body when she was sixteen, the short waist and long legs and moles on her chest, and yet you can hardly remember the men you've slept with, any of them. The names or the bodies, only the faces, just, and the shape, vaguely, of penises, whether they were long, or too thick—God, you dreaded that, the grate of it.

The attendant presents you with a gin and tonic on a silver tray and you look around, startled. The man from the lobby smiles his beautiful boy smile from a distant sun lounger and you lower your head and do nothing more, don't drink, don't look, you're confused and you know that Theo'd be cross at this, a missed opportunity.

Theo. Such a pirate of a woman, with a different energy to her. She's thirsty and needs to drink, it's in the way she walks and listens and leans and talks. She's a woman who *over-lives*, she has so much life in her, it shines under her skin. Does that mean you *underlive*? Your heart dips with panic as if a cloud has skimmed across it.

You look across to the man on the sun lounger now reading his *Tribune* and tilt back your head and close your eyes. You're living your days at the moment how a sheep grazes, meandering, not engaged with anything much. And yet, and yet, you'd never wish for Theo's kind of existence. She's so free, so answerable to no one that she's lost.

The sky deepens, bathers pack up their suntan lotion and one by one leave, the baked breeze stiffens and umbrellas are snapped down for fear they'll cartwheel away. You slip into the pool. The water's ruffled like corrugated iron. You're the only one in it and you slide through the coolness and strike out for the first time in years, feel unused muscles creaking into working order and think of your mother and her strong, confident hands and the ribbons of water when you were seven. You've no family consistently around you now, your friends have become your closest relations: Cole, of course, and Theo, your sister of sorts, although at times there's the intensity of lovers between you.

It's her birthday today, you must call.

You smile as you pull your body through the water and at the end of the pool look up to great plumes of ochre dust blown in from the desert; it's as if the dusk is being hurried centre stage. The attendants move with crisp deliberation now, clearing towels and cushions from chairs. Most people have gone. Palm trees toss their branches like the manes of recalcitrant ponies, twigs and leaves blow into the pool and you climb out of the water at the first fat splats. You smell the earth opening up as if it's breathing, feel the thundery day sparking you alive and you lift your chin to it and inhale deep and gather up, reluctantly, your sun gear. You pass the man from the lobby, still reading valiantly. He looks up at you.

You don't look at him. You walk inside, to your husband, a fluttery anticipation within you.

Lesson 25

<u>lending is, as a rule, the greatest unkindness we can be guilty of, unless we can give</u>

*T*he elderly man who looks after the roses lets you into the room, bowing and smiling his gentle smile. He's presented you, gallantly, with a single stem and you've accepted it graciously; it's a game played with some serious-ness. The petals are deep red, almost black, and you plunge your nose into their oddness: it's a wild plump garden scent from your childhood, not the tight manufactured whiff from the buds you buy at the supermarket. You enter the room sound-lessly, you'll surprise Cole, he'll throw you on the bed and make you laugh and kiss you in his special way and you'll melt, succumb, even though you're still menstruating. Sexy sex, hmm, grubby, spontaneous, impolite kind of sex, you haven't done that for years and all of a sudden it seems necessary. The room's dim from the darkening sky and you can taste the thunder outside and lift your chin to it. Cole's on the phone. You're cross, he shouldn't be doing any work during this trip, he promised.

I can't wait to get out of here, it's driving me crazy, the heat, and he says this in his special voice, *your* voice, but there's a playfulness, a lightness, it's a tone you haven't heard for so long. All she wants to do is run off to the markets and have rides in those fucking carts, I can't stand it, I get so bored, I just want to relax. He pauses. Diz, Diz, no, you can't. He chuckles. Yeah, me too. I'll see you soon, thank God.

Lesson 26

air ventilation oxygen _____

_____

_____

You're very still. You walk past Cole without looking at him. You walk through the French doors, to the veranda, and sit, very carefully, on the wicker chair.

Your thudding heart, your thudding heart.

You sit for a very long time, soundlessly, into the rich silence after the storm. At the end of it the sun feebles out and nothing has cooled down, nothing, it is as hot as it ever was.

2

My soul waiteth on thou more than they that
watch for the morning, I say more than they
that watch for the morning.

—Psalm 130

Lesson 27

The Monday after the return from Marrakech.
A café in Soho, alone. An old London chophouse selling beans
on toast and Tetley's tea in stainless-steel pots, the menu padded
and plastic covered. Reading the paper but not.

Like you are skinned.

I can't explain it, he has said, reddening, every time. When
you've asked him again and again. You're overreacting, he has
said. She's a friend, *our* friend, we'd just have a drink now
and then. And then he stops.

As if what he wants to say can never be said, as if it will
never be prized out. But you will not let up.

Just a friend. Uh huh.

You sit back at his words, you fold your arms. At his explanations that are scattered bits of bone, that are never enough.

You haunt the café in Soho. Want to crawl away from the world, curl up; want to shrink from the summery lightness in the air, the flirty pink on the girls in the streets.

Within this God-tossed time he's never stopped telling you he loves you but you've no desire to listen any more. For the relationship has been doused in a cold shower and you are chilled to the bone with the shock.

Just a friend. Uh-huh.

You will not let up.

Now it's a week since you've known; now two. Everything is changed and nothing is changed, you're reading the paper but not. You prefer this café in Soho over the American coffee chains that seem of late to be everywhere, despite Cole's certain horror at the choice. Before, you'd let his likes and dislikes shape the movement of your day, even when he wasn't with you. But you're disobedient often now, in little ways. For realization of the affair has snapped upon you as fast as a rabbit trap, and you are exiled from your marriage and home and life.

The elderly man behind the till senses something of all

this; he smiles warmly in greeting, now, and hands you your cup of tea without waiting to be asked.

We'd. just. have. a drink. now. and. then. All right?
  I don't believe you. I'm sorry, I can't.
  It's the truth, I am *so sick* of telling you that.
  I don't believe you. *I can't.*
  Your hands hover, frozen, by your head. Your fingers are clawed, your knuckles are bone-white. You have turned into someone else. You do not recognize the voice.

Day after day you shelter in this café in London's red light district. It's a small indication of something that's burst within you. You're not sure why you've picked this place, you never go to cafés or restaurants by yourself, it's too exposing. All you know is that the two people closest to you have gone from your heart, it's flinched shut. And it's only as you spread your newspaper and pour the milk into your tea that you feel the tin foil ball, tight within you, unfurling. No one would guess just by looking at you, the quiet, suburban housewife, that recently in a hotel room in Marrakech your entire future had been crushed by a single blow from a rifle butt.
  And all that's left is rawness, too deep for tears.

She's a friend, just a friend, it's all he can ever say and in this Soho café, the third week of your purgatory, your teacup is slammed down. So hard, the saucer cracks.

Lesson 28

disease is the punishment of outraged
nature

A month after your return from Marrakech. A stagnation sludges up. You're not bored or angry but stopped; nothing engages, nothing interests, you're at a loss over what to do next, with the next hour and with all the days of your life. Sleep is the short-term solution. London's good for that. Its light is milky, filtered, unlike the light from your childhood that stole through the shutters in bold blocks in the morning, nudging you awake and pushing you out. The sky in London is like the water-bowed ceiling of an old house and you doze whole mornings away now and on waking there's a panicky sickness in your gut. Then you walk the streets, seeing but not seeing, husked.

Selfridges lures you inside, its sleek promise. You haven't been here for so long, you used to trawl it with Theo, she'd always have you trying on things you didn't want. You browse the accessories counters. Buy six rings. Space them out on your fingers, blurring your marital status; your engagement and weddings rings are swamped and you smile as you stretch out your hand.

But then it's back, his voice. It always comes back. The tone of it as he spoke to her on the phone. It's not so much the thought of them physically together, it's the intimacy in his voice. It wasn't until you overheard it in the hotel room that you realized how long it'd been since you *had* heard it. And you missed it, violently so.

Your voice.

Your teeth are clenched as you walk to the tube and with effort you soften your jaw and rub at your brow, at a new wrinkle between your eyes. At the end of each night you knead it, your fingertips dipped in the chilly whiteness of Vitamin E cream. Beyond you, the flat ticks. The rooms are dark except for the bedroom. Cole's away a lot now, working late; that's his excuse. There's no light in the hallway to welcome him home. At the end of each night, seated at the dressing table, your fingertips prop your forehead like scaffolding. For it's the long, long nights that defeat you.

When you are blown out like a candle.

Lesson 29

friends are too scarce to be got rid of
on any terms if they be real friends

*T*he buzzer, too loud, blares into your morning. You groan: you're still in bed. The intercom's broken,
you'll have to go down three flights of stairs and open the front
door to find out who it is; in your old bathrobe, without your
face.

Theo. Red lips and red shirt, the color of blood. On her
way to work.

You close the door. This is ridiculous, she says, come on,
we need to talk. You lean your hands on the door with your
arms outstretched. Can't we just talk, she pleads. Her knocks
become thumps, they vibrate through your palms. You
straighten, walk up the stairs, do not look back; your fingers,
trembling, at your mouth.

Theo's betrayal is magnificent, astounding, incomprehensible. It's *her* actions you can't understand, not Cole's. You always assumed she was the one person you'd have your whole life, not, perhaps, your mother or your husband. She's a woman, she knows the rules. Men do not. You're not interested in an excuse, nothing can put it right, for anything she says will be overwhelmed by the violence of the loyalty ruptured and your howling, pummeled heart.

You can't bear to think of them together. You have no idea how Theo is with a man. How she operates, if she turns into someone else; if she changes her manner and voice. It's a side of your girlfriends you've never intruded upon. All you know is that your husband is trapped in her hungry gravitational pull: his voice told you that.

As you were once. Theo was sloppy with your relationship—never turned up to dinner parties with a bottle of wine, never sent thank-you cards, canceled nights out at the last minute, was often late—but she was always forgiven for she made your hours luminous with the gift of her presence; as soon as you saw her all the irritation would be lost.

Now, she tries to contact you again and again but the phone's hung up no matter how quickly she rams in talk, her e-mails are deleted unopened, her letters ripped. You're good at cutting people off, it's always been a skill, a small one but effective; making things neat, moving on. Theo will hate being ignored. It's what she fears most. You feel a strange sense of power, the extreme passivity makes you strong; it's how you can protest, it gives you a voice. Like, sometimes, with sex.

Lesson 30

old medicines should not be kept, as
they are seldom wanted again and
soon spoil

Cole needs you for a party. It's hosted by a
gallery owner with a painting that needs cleaning, a Venetian
landscape by a pupil of Canaletto. Cole's hungry for it; he sus-
pects there's something from the master hidden underneath.
You don't want to go. Don't want to give him anything yet.

Please, Cole says.

I hate that kind of thing. You know that.

Simon likes you. I need this job.

You know the wife Cole wants for this. He's told you before you're good arm candy: everyone likes you, thinks you're
sweet, lovely, wants to chat with you, but it means the
supreme achievement is that everyone is admiring of Cole, for
he's showing off a possession, like a car or a gold watch or a

suit, and you're flavoring people's impressions that he's a success. You'd loved it when he told you this: to be so prized. You've always brought out the best in each other in social situations. At parties your sentences lap over each other as you tell your old anecdotes, at dinners with friends your meals are absently shared, during your own dinner parties it's a smooth double act of cooking and serving and clearing up. You're both good at playing the married couple, you prop each other up.

Please, Cole says now.

All right. All right.

Your hand rests at your throat. You always give in, have done it your whole life; where does it come from, this stubborn need to be liked?

A mews house, not far from your flat. Simon is tall in the center of the crowded room. He judges his success by his proximity to famous people, he name-drops a lot, he can't be by himself. He likes you because you read show business gossip and respond, wide-eyed, to his talk. He's in a relationship, fractiously, with a pop star from Dublin who had a good haircut and a summer Number One whose title you can never recall. She's not at the party. There are no famous people at the party. Simon will be keenly disappointed. You look at all the guests darting eyes over shoulders, mid-conversation, checking out everyone else, it is as if the sole reason everyone is here is to see someone famous.

You want out.

You're alone in a corner on a black leather couch that

creaks like a saddle. There's a lava lamp beside you. It's no longer working. You've never been voracious about partying. You're too good at blushing, and awkward silences, and saying something jarring and wrong. You're not very accomplished with big groups, have always been more comfortable with one on one, the small magic you can work is always dissipated in a crowd. You look at the guests. Hate the thought of being single again, of meeting every man with intent. You redden in front of anyone you're attracted to and have never grown out of it, your body often lets you down. You imagine Theo here with an admiration that hurts: see her sparkling in the center of the room and poking her head into circles of talk and floating from group to group.

You're wearing a black satin dress that has antique kimono panels through its bodice and you usually love this dress but tonight it's wrong, you're overdressed. You have to get back to your flat. You can't walk home by yourself: there are two crack houses on your street and just last week a woman was stabbed. You need Cole. He's in good form, he's working the room; you wish he'd hurry up. You hate the feeling of entrapment you can get at parties, hate being reliant upon someone else for your means of escape. You're stuck, in a black satin dress that tonight is too much.

Cole's with Simon. Neither likes the other much but they keep in touch for they never know when the contact may be useful. They're not talking about the Canaletto, anything but that: it's not Cole's way to be so blunt. There's a lull in the talk and you stand and tell them, politely, you're going home. You walk to the door. A hand is splayed across your lower back. There's steel in it. It propels you to a balcony knotted with people and you shy away but the hand is still firm round your back.

I have to go home, you say, very low, very old.

I just need an address. Five minutes. OK?

You time it, then pull him out.

Cole and you have both won tonight but Cole has won more. He always wins the most.

Lesson 31

<u>children should never sleep with their</u>
<u>heads under the bedclothes</u>

What you're thinking as the two of you walk home, in silence, a foot apart: My husband's name is Cole and that is the most remarkable thing about him, and is it enough? To keep you with him. For doubt has worked through you like poison now, doing its dirty work.

He will never tell you what happened. Perhaps the only chance you had was the afternoon of the hotel room, during the storm, still brittle with the shock of it. And what did you do? You chose to sit, with your thudding heart. Nothing else. For that's always been your way, the retreat, the silence, and it's only later, much later, that you find the words you should have said. But they're never uttered in time, you're too careful of hurting even when hurt, and too cowardly, yes that. You wonder what would happen if you ever let loose with the anger that's silting up your heart. You look across at your husband and know you'll never crack his closed face now, the moment's lost, you've asked him what happened once too often and he's thoroughly sick of your distrust: he's shut up shop, the shutters are rolled down, the lights have been put out. You don't recognize your husband anymore, he's become someone else. A stranger to you, who undresses Theo, bends to kiss her, holds her hips, brushes her closed eyelids with his lips, laughs with her in bed: you shut your eyes for a moment, trying to slam out the thoughts.

Cole opens the front door and strides inside without checking that you're behind him. He goes straight to the bathroom. You stand on the doorstep, staring at the ghost town of a relationship ahead of you and not knowing if you want to step into it. So, it has come to this. In another life you'd be ringing Theo and getting her out of bed, asking if you could crash on her sofa and have a good cry. You imagine her saying of course, Lovebug, of course; you imagine her jumping in her car and collecting you because she doesn't trust you could drive yourself, from the wobble in your voice.

You have nowhere to go.

You don't know what to do.

You have no job, at Cole's insistence, and you feel a hot

little rush of anger at that; how dare he cripple you, how dare he diminish you on purpose.

You step across the threshold. Walk to the bedroom. Sit down at the dressing table, your head bowed, your temples propped.

Lesson 32

<u>a selfish girl's face often looks sour</u>

Mid-July. A burst of audacious heat. Summer has finally begun and you can feel the exuberance on the streets: people are jumping into the fountain at Trafalgar Square and skipping work to lounge on deck chairs in Hyde Park.

Your mood, wine-dark.

You don't have, any more, a sanctuary in kindness and good deeds and surrender; you're changing, you can feel the souring. A thrill plumes through you when couples split, a feeling that order's restored, that it's the way we're all meant to be, alone. You feel a little electric charge when friends lose their jobs or their new magazine's panned, when a baby's miscarried or the heavens hurl rain on a wedding day. What have you become? Unhinged, no longer a doormat, just like everyone else?

But something is beginning to unfold within you. An idea: to live less tentatively, more selfishly. You're intrigued by people who seem foolish and passionate and ridiculous, but *alive* with all the mess that that entails. You've always been too cautious. Too gentle for newsroom journalism, Cole said once, not scary or neurotic enough, thank God.

Trapped by blandness. And fear. And a knowing that it's easier to instruct than to act.

You wonder about those people who just disappear. Theo had a friend who was stuck in a life she didn't want and one day she said I've just got to pop into Tesco and she left her husband in the car park, and never came out. He waited for three hours before raising the alarm.

You wonder about mining a more dangerous seam of yourself. You'd like to try harder to be beautiful, or at least interesting; beauty is power, your mother's taught you that. She'd say for God's sake get rid of those glasses, when you were a teenager, try and make yourself presentable, as if you couldn't possibly be hers.

You glimpse your first gray hair and twang it out, and then you pluck at the tiny almost invisible hairs on your chin and your belly and feel a thrill as they slide out, feel as if your life, your real life, is perhaps beginning. You have to make it begin, you can't just give up. Before, life was something that always seemed to happen to other people. Like Theo.

Lesson 33

A resolution, in mid-August. You have to move beyond this mewly time, all whingy and wrong, you have to haul yourself out. A resolution that some of the momentous issues in a relationship can in the end only be ignored if you want the relationship to survive, they can't be worked through and tossed out. Which is why, perhaps, some people in long-term partnerships have learned to to live with what they don't like. To reclaim the calm. You've seen it in marriages that've weathered infidelity, have seen them contract into a tightness in old age. Do you *want* the relationship to survive?

It's easier to stay than to go.

You can't bear the thought of parties again and singles columns and intimate dinners that don't work, of always trying to find a way to fill up a Friday night. And you were meant to be trying for a baby soon. Cole wants to be a father some day. When you found him it was like a candle to a cave's dark and to throw it all away after you've got to this point, you just can't. You've had the most satisfying relationship of your life with him: you're sure the glow of companionship can come back.

Cole wants the marriage to last. Everything is denied. He doesn't want to bail out.

You don't want Theo to win. Sometimes you fear this consideration drowns out everything else. You can beat her with this; you can't recall beating her at anything.

So, a resolution.

You will live with the silences between Cole and you now. For you've stopped the talk, both of you, you're away in your separate rooms: he in his study, you in the bedroom, too much. At least there's no sex and you're relieved at that, for the memory of it has now distilled to two things: when he didn't come it was frustrating and when he did it was messy, often over your stomach and face, like a dog at a post claiming ownership.

So many ways to live like a prisoner.

But a resolution, to find a way back into a happy life. Although God knows when the fury will soften from you.

You concentrate for the moment on making the flat very beautiful, very spare and pale, like the inside of a white balloon. To *your* taste, for compromise has been lost. You've never dared impose your will so much. The builders come to know a woman who's never been allowed out before, especially with Cole, a woman stroppy, short-tempered, blunt.

And the flat, the beautiful flat, fit for a spread in *Elle*, is as silent as a skull when you enter it.

An emptiness rules at its core, a rottenness, a silence when one of you retires to bed without saying good night, when you eat together without conversation, when the phone's passed wordlessly to the other. An emptiness when every night you lie in the double bed, restlessly awake, astounded at how closely hate can nudge against love, can wind around it sinuously like a cat. An emptiness when you realize that the loneliest you've ever been is within a marriage, as a wife.

Lesson 34

<u>provide yourself with a good stock of
well-made underlinen</u>

The café in Soho. The Friday before the August Bank Holiday. Hot, festively so. A man is at the table beside you, reading a newspaper, *The Times*. You notice the nape of his neck: how odd to be attracted to someone just by a glance at their neck. The hair's black, like the night-time deep in the country.

You're outside on the pavement. A water main has burst nearby and water's spreading lazily across the street. No one seems bothered, yet. Two men and a woman shout and laugh into the water and kick it about, they're in their twenties, they shouldn't be doing this. They're oblivious to their audience and soon drenched.

You smile. Your *Evening Standard* is folded into your bag,

you'll finish it on the tube—God, rush hour, you've left it too late, you'll be standing all the way. You've left it too late because you don't want to be in the flat by yourself, in the silence like a skull. You hate the emptiness when Cole's there and yet when he isn't, too, when he's deliberately out; it's like nothing, now, is quite right in your life. You stand, ready to step into the stream of commuters with their faces anxious for the cloistering of home, and a car careers round the corner and carves through the water, veering away from the trio, and a fan of water arcs up: you're hit. You're stricken, can't move, your mind blanks as if someone has told you a joke and you're meant to get it quick.

You look across to the man next to you. He, too, is wet. You blurt a laugh; here at last is the joke. So does he.

You need some help, you say.

So do you.

You look down. Your white cotton dress is triumphantly wet in a huge patch at the front, it clings like a piece of recalcitrant silk slicked about a tree. You throw back your head and grimace: oh God. And then a man's jacket is wrapped round your shoulders, a man's leading you back to the table, he's holding you in a way that only a husband should hold you: with ownership.

It is, of course, your man with the beautiful nape.

Lesson 35

hooks and eyes

*E*verything is changed.

Gabriel Bonilla, that is his name. You repeat it; the sound is all mealy in your mouth. You smile in apology at that. You must wait until your dress has dried to decency; it may take some time and this Gabriel Bonilla asks if you need to get home straight away—no, it's all right, there's nothing to go home to—and you laugh, too loud, and as it comes out it's as if something within you has cracked.

Well, hello.

So there you are, an hour or two in that greasy spoon of a café and you're both talking about everything and nothing, voices tumbling over the top of each other, learning lives.

Shaking free.

You'd never talk with this freedom, this lightness, if you were unattached. Being married gives you a bloom of certainty, a confidence. But it doesn't stop the blushing. Gabriel Bonilla blushes too, just like you, fully, completely, ridiculously and you dare to think it means something. You're hesitant to ask about a partner and a family, you want to know, must know, but fear the effort of asking will reveal too much, that you'll redden once again. Like after the water splash when you realized he'd seen your body so vulnerably, too many things, the thighs too fat and the nipples through your bra, God, all of it, and your hand flies to your mouth at the recollection but he drops his eyes as if he doesn't want to intrude, as if he's opened a door by mistake to your thoughts.

There's something fascinating about this man sitting before you in his summer-weight suit. You can't quite put your finger on it but it's something decent, old-fashioned, polite. Wrong for this world, for this cram of sex shops and neon lights where a girl languid by a doorway has a junky's spots. This Gabriel Bonilla shouldn't be here. He's from another time, another place; the type of person who wouldn't expect a woman to be driving a car if there was a man in it. There's his Spanish name and yet fluent English—my mother is English, my father Spanish—and again there's your laugh, bursting out; ah ha, so that explains it.

What do you do, you ask.

Guess.

You lean forward, cup your chin in your palm: a teacher, doctor, spy?

I'm an actor, he says.

You sit back. Retract, just a touch. You don't know any actors, you're not sure you want to.

I don't recognize you. Should I?

No, no, he chuckles. No one does, any more. I was famous once, for about a week, in my late teens. I did a dreadful soap—and he holds up his hand at your question, he's not going to divulge—and then two Hollywood films that bombed, and I haven't done much ever since. I now live in terror of appearing on one of those "Where Are They Now?" shows.

You laugh. You've always been distrustful of actors, have suspected that they've never really muddied their paws in the mess of life, they've lived it second-hand. This is unfair but you're suddenly brisk. How on earth do you live, you ask.

Voice-overs. Ads. Foreign video rights. The occasional guest role. And I was sensible when I was young. I bought a flat.

What happens in between? How do you fill up your days?

Let me see, I sleep until one P.M. Have a Scotch for breakfast. Do a line of coke. You both laugh. No, no, I go to the gym and do classes at the Actors Center, go to casting, that type of thing. Read a lot, travel a lot, row, go to the movies, drink too much tea.

You can't grasp a life like this, none of your peers lives as loosely any more. This Gabriel Bonilla answers your questions as if he's answered them a thousand times before and he couldn't care less. The lack of concern over welfare and career path and what he's doing with his life is intriguing, silly, odd. He strikes you as a man who's not hungry for anything, he has a flat and enough money to get by; there's no need to grasp or to rush. It's not unattractive, this lightness. Then he says he's working on a script about something else he's addicted to and you lean forward: what, come on, tell me?

Bullfighting.

The gulp of a laugh. You stuff the little girl down, sit on the lid of her box.

Bullfighting?

He's laughing too, his father was a matador but he was never much of a success because he wasn't suicidal enough, he liked his life too much. His father only ever fought in provincial rings but he's got an idea for a film, he's told his family he's finally embarking on a proper life and he's burying himself in London's wonderful libraries, the world's best, and he's up to his ears in research. He's writing in them, too, because he'd go mad if he didn't get out. You examine his hands, long and lean, like a priest's, you take them in yours and he tells you the strength in a matador's wrist is what they rely on to make their mark and your hands slip under his and try to encircle them like two rowlocks for oars and you feel their weight, clamp them, soft.

Are your father's anything like these, you ask.

Absolutely. The spitting image. I also have his cough. And his laugh.

But they're so thin, you tease, they couldn't kill a bull!

It's not about aggression or force. Oh *dios mio*, you have so much to learn, and his head is bowing down to his palms still in yours.

How did it get to this, so suddenly, so quickly? You sit back. Look at him. The lower lip puffy, pillowed, ripe for splitting. The long, black lashes like a child's. The tallness in the seat, the slight self-consciousness to it, as if he was mocked, perhaps, at school. The body kept in shape. There's a beauty to him, to his shyness, his decency, you've never been with a man who has a beauty to his body, it's never mattered, you've never cared about that enough. You imagine this Gabriel Bonilla naked, your palm on his chest, reading the span of it and the beating heart, and you cross your legs and squeeze your thighs and smile like a ten-year-old who's just been caught with the last of her grandmother's chocolates.

I'll take you to a bullfight some day, he says. You'll love it, I promise.

You feel the heat in your cheeks, you try to still it down, you see the heat in his too. You recognize his shyness for you've always been shy yourself. You rarely see shyness in a man, it's always disguised as arrogance, abruptness, aloofness. You're too alike, this Gabriel and you. You recognise it in the way he doesn't sit quite comfortably in the world, can't quite keep up. A jobbing actor, still, and he's OK with that. He smiles, right into your eyes, you're distracted and all your questions are suddenly wiped out. He turns the conversation back upon yourself, interviews you as if he's trying to extract the marrow of your life: your marriage, flat, family, job, colleagues, boss. You answer openly, easily, talk slips out smooth, it's all ripe with a dangerous kind of readiness, a lightness is singing within you.

But you tell yourself you will never spoil it all by sleeping with him, will never have the connection stained by that. You don't want sudden awkwardness, don't want sour sleeper's breath in the morning or unflushed toilets and smoker's breath or farts. It took you a year to fart when Cole was in an adjoining room, two to fart in the same room. You sometimes bite the inside of your mouth so furiously that blood's drawn and the rabbity working of your lips is a private, peculiar thing that no one but Cole ever sees. You cut your toenails in front of him, wear underwear that's falling apart, defecate, piss. You open yourself to your husband in a way you don't for anyone else but perhaps he knows too much: all the magic's been lost.

Cole.

You used to talk like this with him once, when you were lovers just starting out. You don't want Gabriel Bonilla ever to be disappointed in you, to drift before anything's begun. So the situation will be preserved just exactly as it is, like a secret document that's tucked deep into a pocket of your wallet, always hidden, always close, that you can take out and dream about at will, a safe's combination, a treasure map, a prisoner's plan of escape.

Gabriel takes out a fountain pen that opens with a click as agreeable as a lipstick. He scribbles down a number on the back of the bill. A man hasn't given you his number for so long. What does it mean, what comes next, is he playing with you, is it a game? And when your fingers brush you draw back, too quick.

He *knows* you're married. He says he'd like to meet Cole. Which throws you.

Lesson 36

happiness and virtue alike lie in action

_O_n the tube hurtling home your fingers worry at the slip of paper like an archaeologist with a snippet at a dig. Connections like this happen so rarely, once or twice in a lifetime perhaps. You would have seized it once, when you were young; you would have dreamt it was the kernel for a big, consuming love, perhaps. But now? A tall, shy, out-of-work actor who's about your age and yet seems somehow unformed, as if he hasn't quite stepped into life. A drifter and a dreamer, hanging by the phone, hostage to his agent, always living by the will of someone else.

Everything Cole is not.

    With his days to himself.

You smile. You hold the paper to your lips as if you're anointing it. You'll call tomorrow, just hello, as a friend, just that. You feel like you've dived into the shallow end of a cold pool in one foolhardy zoom but it's all right, you haven't cracked your spine; you can smile as you power through the resistance, your body peels away from the danger, you've survived the risk.

Everything is changed and you feel shawled by that, anticipation wraps itself around you, a thrill at the secret, secret thought of him.

Lesson 37

Where were you all night?

The movies.

What did you see?

Some Iranian thing, you'd hate it.

Hmm.

Cole's eating a bowl of Heinz tomato soup at the
kitchen bench, a weekend jumper over his business shirt.
The fridge is now a tomb for items with strange smells and
growths: mouldering cheese, blue-speckled bread, jars of
tomato paste hosting a soft pale fur. Neither of you has
cared enough lately, the oven's used to store pots and pans,
it's been a long time since a Sunday roast. There was such
a tenderness to your little home, once: Theo used to drop

in often, unexpected, as if she was cleaving herself to its warmth.

Now, Cole and you have stopped trying. You dreaded that once, that as a couple you'd stop the offers of a bath run or a cup of tea or the dishes done. Actually, it's survivable. The opposite of love isn't hate, it's indifference. Indifference emotionally, indifference physically. You haven't made love since the hotel room of fresh roses every two days, but tonight you kiss him on the crown of his head and let your lips linger and it wakens something in your groin.

I'm going to bed, you say.

Hmm, again; deep in *The Simpsons* and the soup.

He doesn't seem to notice your gesture, or doesn't want to buy into it right now: *The Simpsons* has ten minutes to go.

You smile. You don't care. For you've walked back into the sun, it's warm on your back. You have a new friend in your life, to play with, to be young again with, to wake you up.

Lesson 38

<u>a cold bath will enable a person to</u>
<u>sleep who otherwise cannot</u>

Cole stays up late, it's not unusual, he's often gone to bed at a different time from yourself. He's at his laptop most likely, trawling for porn. He was embarrassed when you first caught him, several years ago: he snapped down the screen. Now all he does is turn the computer away. The stutter of a courtesy, and it's not enough.

Cole told you once, early on, that he stayed up late because he liked the bed warm, you're my hot-water bottle, he'd said and you'd giggled and licked him behind the ear. You used to think your husband wasn't near as churning and smudged as yourself but even: clean, open, uncomplicated. Now you know there's a secret life you know nothing of and never will, and no one knows anyone's secret life.

You see him more clearly now. A man who's glided through his adulthood with the serenity and distance of someone who doesn't want any questions too close. He hides behind a mask of absolute calm, it gives the impression that he's always reserving his energy for someone else. He seems comfortable with his lot, maybe he's happy, maybe not. No one ever really asks him. He's happy to maintain a slight gap between himself and the world and not give himself away too much.

You, now, want to be pushed up close. You no longer want the marriage retreat, the little bubble of togetherness that was so cozy once.

You'd visit Cole's studio in the early days and sit on a high stool among the easels and palettes and harsh, blue-white lamps, the bottles of white spirits and surgical gloves. The room smelt of oil paints and varnish and turps, and had the clutter of a cobbler's shop. You loved the man hidden underneath who emerged so spectacularly in this private space. His apron over his business shirt, sleeves carefully rolled, was always spattered with plaster and paint.

He was working at the time on an early nineteenth-century portrait of Madame Recamier, a renowned French beauty of her day. The canvas was flat on a heated table, to soften the surface, and he talked you through it as he bent over it. She was brought up in a convent and married off at sixteen to a wealthy banker. The union was never consummated; there was a rumor that her husband was really her father. Cole told you, as he worried her pale cheek with a cotton-tipped spatula, that to compensate for the desert of the marriage she used her looks to snare dozens of men, but remained a virgin her entire life.

She was cursed by every single bastard who fell in love with her, he said, standing and assessing the bright square of his work. She had this incredible calm about her. They all fell for it.

I can see it, you said. In her smile.

You watched your husband bend over the crazed surface of the canvas with the care of a stonemason at the block, clearing away the soot and grime until Madame Recamier's face and then body glowed pale before you both. You were transfixed by his fingers that fussed with the attentiveness of love, bringing to life the lips, just the lips, in one golden afternoon, the pale swell of her breast in another.

Cleaning is always the riskiest part of the process, he told you. It's all so unknown. What you find underneath might be magnificent, or something you just want to throw out. You never know.

You could watch him and listen to him forever in those days: you loved the seductiveness of a man deep in work. You knew, then, it was a reciprocated love and it was a canopy of joy over your life.

You see your husband now. A man who hides in art, and porn, who's nourished by an interior world you know nothing of. His work is a world you can never really be a part of, he burrows away into it, just as he does with his moated, secret life.

Why did you marry him?

Because he said yes. And you'd reached the stage where

you never expected any man to want you that much. And he was such a good friend, right from the beginning, he was a mate; never one of those lovers where you wondered what you had in common apart from sex. And there's the deep urge within you as your thirties gallop on, the furious want.

Give me children or else I dye, wrote the anonymous Elizabethan author of your old book.

Oh yes.

Cole has a favorite photograph of you, he says it reveals your secret self. It was taken for a magazine article about bright young things, the ones to watch, and their mentors. You'd been chosen by an old student of yours, now an ITV news reader, a hungry young woman who'd straightened her West Country vowels and had a meteoric rise from the local Bristol paper into prime-time TV. There was also a celebrated violinist, a geneticist, an architect, a novelist.

You didn't want to do it but didn't say no, of course: it was good publicity for your faculty. You'd never actually liked her enough, had been jealous and a little afraid of her steely greed to succeed. She hid her determination within friendliness and flattery but you saw straight through it.

The photographer was Colombian. He was exasperated with you all, wanted the group to relax. He asked you to think of the most sensuous thing you could imagine and yell it out, and there was uncomfortable laughter and then silence.

Skin to skin said your former student suddenly. Someone else, foie gras. The softness of a baby's thighs. Swimming, naked, at midnight. The smell of freshly cut grass. Fauré's 'Sanctus'. A girlfriend's laugh.

Until there was only you left.

Kissing the back of your husband's neck, you said, while he was absorbed in his work. Your voice stumbly and hesitant, your blush deep. The photo was taken and when it was published it was all, still, in your face.

Cole loved your look, he knew it well but had never seen it caught.

He had no recollection of you ever kissing his neck while he was at work.

Lesson 39

<u>there should not be overcrowding in bedrooms</u>

Night, bed, alone, and the glare of what's happened during that meeting with Gabriel is imprinted in your head like the too-bright fluorescent lights that were never switched off in your school's corridors. Cole's fallen asleep on the couch in front of the television. You cannot sleep, cannot sleep, and then it's dawn. Love is attention and you're not getting any: you're like a balloon that's jerked free from the fist holding it down and is now climbing and swerving in a choppy sky.

You think of other things, in bed, alone. They're with you most nights, to lull you to sleep. A group of men watching you being penetrated by a broom handle. You don't know any of the perpetrators very well. It's never intimate or tender. It's filmed. Sometimes women will be watching the penetration; by candlesticks, by animals, sometimes the women will be participating. And the men. Hands will be running over your naked body, parting your legs, probing, slipping inside. Almost every night you imagine these things to drop you into sleep. The movies in your head were most vivid during your teenage years, you can still remember the effect twenty years later, the intensity of them. And now, following the afternoon of Gabriel, you're vastly awake and holding your fingers snug between your legs and wanting to feel again with the spark of those teenage years, wanting that combusting under your skin.

You want to ring Theo, you miss your confidante, it's a huge silence in your life. She was the only person you ever felt comfortable ringing beyond ten. You'd talk sex with her endlessly, what you wanted, what you didn't; all the things you never said to a man. You loved her expression to describe a good fuck—dirt—meaning it'd be dirty, it'd be sexy sex. A man who's dirt, you'd always loved the idea of that. And sexy sex.

Now, alone, you're bound by caution. Have you ever acted, as an adult, exactly as you wished? You've been battened down for so long; the good teacher, friend, wife. And you're most passive in bed, all surrender and wanting to please so much. Your fantasy life has never leaked into your real life. But in bed, now, alone, possibility is putting its key in the lock, like a stream of desert light in the morning, luring you out.

Cole stumbles into the room at five and presses his body into you, as if he's trying to draw the warmth from your flesh. You shrug him off.

Lesson 40

there are few who willfully injure their
health, but many thoughtlessly destroy it

*T*en A.M.

You reach for your handbag, hope you're not ringing too
soon, don't even know what to say, just hello, will that do,
and I wanted to say thanks for the other day; you've rehearsed
it, the lightness in your voice. You're living more boldly, you're
beginning, and Theo's words sound in your head: it's no use
waiting for the light to appear at the end of the tunnel, you
just have to stride down and light the bloody thing yourself.
There's nothing wrong with a new friend for there seem to be
less and less as the years roll over in your narrowing life.

Ten A.M. and your thudding heart, your thudding heart.

The slip of paper isn't there.

You're scrabbling through your wallet and searching the

floor and the steps and the ground outside but it's gone and your fingers are dragging through your hair and your teeth are tearing at your nails, there's no phone number under directory enquiries and you have no address, of course, and then you sit on the hallway floor, your head thrown back against the wall, for a very long time, very still, in the flat, with its silence like a skull.

He's gone.

As if chunks have been ripped from the book of your future.

You can't move, your whole life feels slumped: you don't know what to do next. You sit there for so long, your hand tucked into your knickers, against your bare flesh. When you withdraw your fingers you stare at the glutinous shine on them, the shout of it. You gasp, your hand trembles; a teenager all over again, so abruptly.

But you have no number, no address. And he doesn't have yours. He is gone.

You feel drained. It took so much effort to get to this point, to overcome the nausea and nerves, to resolve to pick up the phone. You didn't realize how much you were counting on the possibility of him, a new something to fill your life, until he was lost.

Lesson 41

remember to walk briskly and not
saunter about or be forever peering
into shop windows

$\mathbf{Y}$ou return to the café in Soho, alone,
through September, through October, and he never comes
back.

On a Monday of cold sunshine a young woman is beside
you. She's reading the sex issue of *The Face* magazine; she's
strongly by herself, as if this café is her office and she's been
this at ease in her skin her whole life. You wish you could be
that. You buy *The Face* on the way home, flushing as the
newsagent takes your money. You'll never go back to his shop,
you're not that young woman.

That night, alone, in the bedroom, words you've never heard before:

Californicate: copulating shamelessly in every possible position. Chili dog: defecating on a woman's chest, then masturbating with her breasts. Daisy chaining: a number of people connecting through oral sex. Flooding the cave: urinating into a partner's vagina. Hum job: oral sex given to a man while humming a tune. On and on and you close the magazine and smooth the cover down, you place it in the bottom of your bedside drawer, you check it's well tucked.

Repelled. Horrified. Wet.

Thinking of the woman in the café, and the man who never came back. Thinking of anonymous, uncomplicated sex. Arousing yourself with it all, now, rather than sedating yourself into sleep; wanting it in your life.

Lesson 42

The next day at the café you're like an anemone unfurling within the silky coaxing of the water because you've decided that for the next six months you'll live your life differently from the way you've ever lived it before: indulgently, selfishly, willfully, before marriage and motherhood close over you. You dream of no commitment to anything but your own pleasure, you dream, with renewed vigor, of finding a satisfying fuck. If you'd ever have the courage for that.

You were a serial sleeper once, during your final year of university, propelled by the thought of launching yourself into the world without any experience of men, a virgin at twenty-two and full of shame and self-loathing at the fact.

You had an innocence then, in your early twenties. You

could pass as sixteen, as still needing to be taught, your face hadn't yet settled. So one Saturday night at a friend's you became drunk and emboldened, you had to get it done. There was a man next to you in the doorway; he was taller than you, had clear skin, he'd do. Everyone else was deep into a double episode of *The Young Ones*, they'd never notice you'd gone.

You took a deep breath: do you want to go upstairs, you asked.

What, he said, leaning close.

Let's go upstairs, come on.

You took his hand; he had no idea of your pounding heart. You never saw him again, didn't want to, his name was quickly lost. There were many after that. They were always snatching the bait, thinking it was you, in fact, who'd fallen prey and not realizing that the girl with the face who needed to be taught had become a collector, an archivist of sexual experiences. All disappointing; too dry, painful, anticlimactic, fumbling, bleak.

So you tried something else. An older man. Your neighbor, a graphic designer who'd never settled down. The age difference was nineteen years. It was worse. He was from an era when sex was purely for the man's satisfaction; he thought a good fuck was just hammering away vigorously while you lay there and thought of England; he thought condoms were a joke. He told you afterward as he rubbed your flat belly that he could never sleep with a woman over thirty, he didn't like them enough: the sagging skin on their necks, the lines on their faces, the bodies thickening out. But you know another reason, now; because by then women have lost their docility, they have awareness, they know too much.

And they want things themselves.

So, nothing sparked. Theo, meanwhile, seemed to be sailing her way through men and through life. For you the best moment was always the anticipation, the thrill of giving the men what they wanted and as soon as the clothes were off something was lost. It always seemed to be two people connecting but utterly failing at it, too, and there was a gulf of loneliness in that, and after several years you gave up and slipped into your dream world every single night. So your twenties passed.

Whenever you did make love it was your thoughts that stirred you more than the touch of the man. He never knew that he wasn't at the center of your focus while he was on you, that he was merely kick-starting the film in your head. As he pushed inside you'd slip into concentrating on a scenario that would trigger your pleasure. It all had little to do with the person making love to you. You never found the sex sexy; maybe it would come with the next man or the next but it never combusted for you. What was all the fuss about?

You were much better at it by yourself, in your head.

Lesson 43

What you want:

The lights turned off. A touch that's gentle, slow, provocative, that builds you up, that makes you want it too much. An orgasm; it doesn't have to be at the same time as the man, just one orgasm so that you know what everyone's talking about. Eye contact. A quick coming that's not on your breasts or your face. Holding afterward, skin to skin. Oral sex, precisely where you ask, for as long and as soft and as slow as you'd like. Sex that's uncomplicated, with no ties, where the man will do exactly what you want. Claiming happiness for yourself: you're so used to focusing on your partner's pleasure at the expense of your own.

What you do not want:

To suck a penis. The smell of stale smoke. A tongue in your ear. Underwear involving satin or g-strings or leopard print or lace. The vaginal sex to go on too long. A thrusting so hard that it burns, it hurts. Swallowing. Breast sucking, breast licking, breast anything. To be asked *what are you thinking*. For it to be pushed upon you when you're tired, grubby, not yet wet. Being pinned down. A rush to get in. A penis that's too big. Loud snorting at climax, or groaning, or any expression like "ooh yes, baby" and "c'mon." For the roll-over after the coming to be too abrupt. To be kicked out too quick.

What you love:

The arch of the foot, its bones, rake-splayed. Wide, blunt, clean fingernails. Michelangelo wrists. Cleanliness. The nape of your neck nuzzled. Your eyelids kissed. Burrowing deep under the blankets. Clothes to be drawn off slowly, in exquisite anticipation. Cold, smooth walls you are rammed against. The sound of a lover's breath close to your ear. Your hair pulled back when he's inside. Your name spoken aloud just before he comes. Connecting, a holiness fluttering within you both. Seduction that's slow, intriguing, unique, by flattery, extravagant gestures, text: poem scraps on napkins, filthy e-mails that should never be sent, love letters scrawled on Underground passes, a line composed in lipstick on your back as you sleep, written backward, to be read in the mirror; oh yes, all that.

Lesson 44

if you have a dog and never let him out the poor fellow will bark and howl miserably

Cole has a gift. He hasn't given you one for so long, since Marrakech, when you received chocolates and magazines and jewelry from the souks. You protest but you're smiling, you can't help it, for it signals a thaw, a softening back into an easier way. You can both feel it, time is smoothing things out. You both want this.

It's an envelope. You slide your fingers beneath the heavy, cream flap.

Private membership to the London Library. The writers' library. It's too ironic, heartbreaking, apt and your heart swells with light and guilt. Your husband's blackmailing you with generosity and you know exactly what you'll do, for a writers' library might, just might, have an actor in it, who's researching a screenplay, perhaps.

I thought it might give you a kick start, Cole says. For the book.

Ah, the book.

For you'd told him once that one day you'd like to take your cheeky seventeenth-century text and do something with it. It was one reason why he was so insistent you give up the drudgery of teaching, to try something you'd always wanted to do—although sometimes you suspected it was just to keep you all to himself. You'd showed him the section where the author stated that women married not for pleasure but for the propagation of children; and her conclusion that the wives of barren men should be allowed to sleep with other men fit and lusty. Isn't that gorgeous, you remember teasing him, when can I start? And Cole had grabbed you firmly by the arm and had smacked you, stingingly, on the bum.

The cupboard. Quick.

And you'd laughed and laughed.

You'd told Cole that there was a novel in the text, or a history perhaps, the intimate kind that cracks open private lives. It felt good to tell him, as if it would give some weight to your own life. You're not sure, now, though, you ever really meant it.

But he didn't forget.

No one except your husband knows of the cautiousness at the heart of your life. Your adulthood has been a progressive retreat from curiosity and wonder, an endless series of delays and procrastinations. You wanted to be so much, once, but life kept on getting in the way. You shone during your journalism degree but were never quite hungry enough for a newsroom. You dreaded the cold calling, of intruding so much on people's lives. You did an MA and drifted into teaching and were always doubting your abilities: said *shouldn't it be someone else* when your colleagues urged you to apply for a higher post, asked *me? Really?* when offered a promotion, never pushed for a pay raise. You settled. Shunned creativity, flight, risk, never had the courage to give a dream, any dream, a go.

And now you hold the envelope to your lips and smile and kiss your husband on the forehead. You'll go to the Library tomorrow, you say it's the perfect gift. You don't tell him you'll be looking for a man in a very neat suit, with a beautiful nape. For Cole is seducing you with thoughtfulness and you want him to know how grateful you are.

But something is all skittery within you and there's the light and the guilt of that.

You know what Theo would do in this situation. You wonder about your Elizabethan wife. If she ever acted on her words, if she was that courageous, or stupid. Indulgent. Selfish. Bold.

Lesson 45

God helps those who help themselves

The London Library arrests time, it drags you into its rich dark depths and holds you there, captive and absorbed and lost. You find a space to write in the old encyclopedia room; it has discreet plugs for laptops embedded in the floor. Your little volume sits demurely on your desk, with its shiny coffee-colored leather cover and broken clasps. And its shocking declarations in their firm, neat hand.

Eve be more excellent than Adam. Eve be less sinful than Adam.

A husband they desired to have, not so much to be accounted wives, as to be made mothers. For they know that woemen should be saved by childbearing.

Where, know yee, shall we finde a man be he ever
so old, barren, weak and feeble that hathe been so
kind and curteouse to his wife that was willing to sub-
stitute another more able man in his place, that his
wife might have issue.

Woemen bare rule over men.

Why was the author compelled to write such things? What is the remoteness, the chafing within you? Why do you always do things you don't want to, now that you're embedded in this relationship? You tolerated so much before, within the glow of new love, now you don't. Why do you feel stronger and more serene when you're by yourself, that you don't want your husband around too much? Everyone's always considered you an excellent candidate for the role of wife; you're compliant and companionable, you endure, with feigned enthusiasm, in-law dinners, action films, client drinks. If only they knew of the restlessness within you, the tapping at your elbow, the tugging at your skirt.

You're not sure what to do with the book, it's like walking under water when you try to find a way in. But it will come. And there are many distractions—magazines and newspapers and the Internet and the looking for Gabriel, always that.

Especially in the Reading Room, at lunch hour, just in case.

The space is joyous with light from tall windows and hushed with cerebration, thick with an atmosphere of scholarship and sleep. Several old leather armchairs are in a line, in stately repose, their bellies now grazing the floor. You get to know the regular visitors. The beautifully dressed elderly man who places a white linen handkerchief on a seat before taking a very long time to lower himself into it. The large man always asleep, head thrown back, mouth agape, hands crossed protectively over a book on his chest like a dead man's Bible placed by a widow. The mousy woman who arrives promptly at noon every day and kneels on the floor by a reading man and rests her head on his knees. His fingers sift, absently, through her hair and they don't speak for half an hour and then they leave and your heart fills with tenderness for what they have together as a couple—for you had it once—and then tightens for what, perhaps, they'll become.

The library gives you a feeling of industriousness, props your life. You dress as if going to work; you're not the only one doing this. A middle-aged man in a pinstriped suit does nothing but read *The Times* every day from cover to cover and you guess an unsuspecting wife is behind the creamy stiffness of his collars and cuffs, and wonder how long he can sustain it.

Soon you're frequenting the library ravenously, you want it every day, just as you needed your café, once. In the cram of London, amid its grubby, muscular energy, the narrow building is a refuge and a tonic. And always, you're searching. For you're infected by the idea of Gabriel and you feel, with an odd certainty, that he will come.

Lesson 46

lazy, stay-indoors persons frequently
have diseases

The library's computer room, where you write e-mails to your friends and trawl the newspapers for show business gossip: the latest marriages that have crumbled, the best and worst gowns from recent award ceremonies, Hollywood pregnancies, arrests. You're sitting at a desk with your shoes flipped off and knees drawn up—it has something to do with wanting to be young again, with living a more vivid life.

A man peers playfully over your shoulder, trying to read what you're reading and you look up, startled. He asks if you'd like to come for a drink with some of the regulars after work. You look around the room, at the six other people in it and realize they all know each other, it's a gang. Instinctively you begin to say no, it's always your way to refuse the second cup of tea, the seat on the tube, the drink after work. But something, this time, makes you stop.

Yes, I'd love to.

The man smiles. He glances at your wedding ring, perhaps, among your jumble of rings. You look at him as if for the first time. Prematurely balding, with his hair clipped close to his scalp. Wearing luxurious black velvet trousers that sit oddly with a striped shirt. Younger than what you'd first imagined, weeks ago, from a distance, better-looking than what you'd dismissed him as. You know in a second you'd never sleep with him, it's a mental game you play with every man you meet. It's not just the velvet, he's not your type. He won't make your lip tremble, won't draw a blush, won't make you seize up. You smile at him warmly; you can relax.

Lesson 47

every girl can dance and should learn
to do it well

There are three men and a woman at the pub and swiftly you're telling them more than you ever intended, eager for contact, slightly drunk. They know nothing of you. It's exhilarating, like moving to a foreign country where no one knows of your past; you can make yourself up as you go. As you explain your book you become authoritative, confident, witty, brisk, and plans for the project spark as you speak. You talk of the obedient wife writing secretly, late at night, galloping her pen through page after page and hiding it away when she hears her husband at the door and opening her Bible and stilling her face with her fingertips on her flushed cheeks. Hinting to her lover that she's writing a book, for she has to have a lover; yes, yes, she must.

Her husband finds out. He drags her by the hair to the cupboard and locks her in, he shuts his hands over his ears at her cries; she begs him for mercy, he does not speak. Eventually, over many days, her screams become whimpers, they die out. The lover never knows what happens. He's told by her maidservant the wife has been sent to a harsh and distant nunnery; he can't find her, he searches the breadth of the land. And he never knows if she really loved him, or if she was making it all up. He dies a broken man. As does the husband.

Perhaps, perhaps.

Tonight works, magnificently. The group doesn't have to know you'll be going home to a very still flat. You watch, astounded, the woman you've become, insisting on the next round and then asking when they'll be meeting next.

Tomorrow, says your man in the velvet trousers. Most nights, in fact.

I'll see you then; and you're out the door quick, as if you're off to something else. The sense of the illusion, triumphantly executed, buoys you down the street.

Lesson 48

to know right is well, but to do right
is better

The following Sunday.

You flick through the newspapers' magazines. Stop at
Theo's column. Since Marrakech you've not been able to read
it, until now. You've been slipping that section into the bin before Cole gets a chance to look.

This week, it's the usual kind of queries:

Dear Dr. Theo, my new boyfriend's getting frus-
trated. He loves me on top during sex but I feel so
self-conscious; it just makes me freeze. It's driving
him crazy as he says he's the only one making any
effort.

Dear Frozen, ah, yes, sex on top. It can be wonderful, but only if you're completely uninhibited with how you look. If you're at all body conscious, it's an extremely vulnerable position for a woman to be in. So, what to do? Well, girl, you need to get used to some friendly, relaxed nudity with your boyfriend. If that's too big a step for now, why don't you try wearing one of his shirts? Men usually love that.

Dear Dr. Theo, my ex-husband took forever to climax and I worry I didn't provide him with enough grip. Could it be possible that my vagina is just too big?.

Dear Worried, you know what, maybe your ex just liked to savour the whole experience. Did you ever ask? We girls just don't ask enough, you know! But some simple exercises can strengthen your pelvic floor muscles—to find out where they are, try halting the flow when you're on the toilet. If you do them regularly, you'll be able to grip your men deliciously tight!

You always read her columns because she expected you to but never really applied them to your life; they were good for a giggle, that's all. Your mother looked out for them voraciously. It always seemed slightly obscene to you that a postmenopausal woman would enjoy them so much. She was devastated when you told her that Theo made up most of the letters.

———————

But then, but then, to a question about a lover who's providing great sex, and is that enough to leave her husband and two kids, Theo writes in stern, condemning response:

> *No, it's not enough. And just remember, its a strong person who has the courage to end a relationship that isn't working, before embarking on a fresh one. Its a weak person who cheats on someone.*

Your heart pounds as you read. You push the magazine into the bin. How dare she write that; how dare she publicly pretend she's squeaky clean; someone else. And whom is she writing that for? Cole? You, to throw you off the scent? Women are so accomplished at battling in subtle, ingenious, covert ways; at clothing their betrayers' fingers in the smoothest of kid. And it's usually other women they're competing with, not men.

Lesson 49

paraffin is highly inflammable

You ration your evenings with the writers to once, perhaps twice, a week; it doesn't seem right, as a wife, to be out every night. Cole was amused when you'd told him of the gatherings; he felt it was a new hobby for you, a way to open out your life. You'd been careful to tell him all the men were attached, with boyfriends or girlfriends or wives.

A Friday night. There are eight of you in the pub; you've all come from the library with your laptops and papers in shoulder bags. And then another man appears and the group exclaims and arms reach out.

He reddens, to see you, and the rest of them look at you afresh. The new persona dissolves in an instant, in that moment of seeing him, you're back to your old self: your top lip trembles in its greeting.

We know each other, Gabriel says, quizzing you with his eyes.

How's it going? Your voice is hoarse, the three words are all you can push out.

He's just popped by for a drink and the rest of the group want to know how he is and where the hell he's been and when is he going to get a computer and enter the twenty-first century like everyone else. You stand back and watch. You're struck, again, by the peculiar gentleness, the shyness, still. He's been in LA, at some castings for pilot season, it's where all the English actors end up around this time of year, and then he stopped off in Rome and there was Barcelona too, a family wedding, and he speaks politely and affably but he'd much prefer to talk about something else. You recognize it; he's not good in big groups. You're struck, again, by the hair washed in night and the small clearing behind his ear, its vivid white. You want to lick it. You tighten your inner thighs as he leans across you to the bar, to pay for his wine, not beer like the rest. Another suit, of course, as if it would never cross his mind to wear anything else, as if he always visits his mother and attends church. No one in your life attends church. The suits have a vintage line to them; maybe they're his peculiar

135

style, or they're his father's, or he's poorer than you thought. There's so much to ask.

He doesn't bother fitting in with everyone else. Why shouldn't he wear a suit and write in longhand and disappear for several months? He's a man very loved; he's like a rock that's been struck by the sun for a long time and is warm with it. You see him as the only boy in his family with many adoring older sisters, the late child, the lovely mistake: there's none of the responsibility or gravity of an eldest child. There's such a sweetness to him. It's all in his smile.

Your breathing is wrong, it's all jerky and light, you cannot still it. The others joke about the screenplay that's taking a bloody long time to complete.

A woman called Martha jumps in. You've noticed her a lot: she walks with a heavy brow, as if her fists are clenched. She teases that Gabriel's finished twenty-eight pages and they're the work of a genius but they've taken eleven months to produce and there's doubt among the rest of them that another twenty-eight will ever be completed, and you can see in that moment you're not the only one caught.

What's it called, you stumble the words out.

I don't know, yet.

His boyish beam, his shrug. You want to get away from this bar, it's all stilted and jostly and wrong. He's blushed upon seeing you and it must mean something and you make an effort to still your breathing and a sip of wine slips into a gulp. One by one the others are drifting away, even Martha, lingering Martha, and finally, finally you're alone. Silence, for a moment, then laughing from you both.

Well.

Well.

You apologize for not calling, tell him you lost his number and were terribly upset and then hate yourself for revealing that. But he's flattered, delighted, in fact. I'm glad you were miserable, he says, it makes me feel good. And you look at him, trying to work him out: he's not interested in shielding himself.

Then the talking, an hour or two or thereabouts, everything and nothing, the way Cole and you used to talk, in the giddy time following the first fuck when the friendship had burst into something else. The time when you'd fuck greedily, when you'd tail off with exhaustion at the wilting end of one night and pick it all up again the next. When the more sex you had the more you wanted as all the rusty cogs within you were oiled up. Before familiarity and exhaustion and stress wound you down and the less you had, the less you wanted. And you stopped.

You'd never want that to happen with Gabriel.

He's making you feel so alive, just being around him. You've always loved people like that: heart lifters, not heart sinkers. He's making you laugh again, with your eyes. You talk as if this is the last time you'll ever talk and there's so little time and you need to know everything, now, before it's too late.

How did it go, in LA?

I don't know. I never know. I'm always being told I was second-best. The list of failures is very long.

There's no anger, frustration, angst; maybe the affability is an extremely smooth defense but you suspect your Gabriel is not very good at pushing his way through life. Is it such a bad thing? Everyone's so good at seizing now, especially Theo; her life is all about hunting down the best deals, perks, sales, nothing rare and desirable escapes the vigor of her grasp. Gabriel is content to let all the grabbing slip by him. He has a sunniness in his character that makes you want to protect him and preserve what he's got.

When he listens, his head leans on one side. He says *interesting* after your sentences a lot; savoring what you say. He's hungry to know you. You used to be like that once, with strangers, at dinner parties and weddings and blind dates, you had the zeal of a collector then, firing off questions and hiding yourself. Before it was all buried in the cotton wool of complacency, and Cole, and you weren't near as interested in anyone else. Gabriel wants to know what you think, he's giving you space in the conversation: it's refreshing in a man. You're responding like a neglected child at the back of the class who has a new teacher and flowers under the attention. And turns into someone else.

He's making you feel beautiful. Wanted. Confident. Unique. Cole never sees you as any of that, he loves to tell you how you are, what you're like; to box you up tight.

At the end of the night you say good-bye to Gabriel—no kiss, just a brush of warm cheek—and you walk down the street propelled by a zinging high, it's as if you could leap and brush the sky. You have his number and he has yours and on the tube, once again, you anoint his slip of paper with your lips.

This one you will not lose.

Lesson 50

<u>putting damp sheets on a bed is little short of murder</u>

A light under the front door. You're usually home first—you sober your face down. Cole asks where you've been and you say the library, it opens late on Wednesdays, remember? Good, he says, I'm glad you're getting something out of it. He looks up from his *Evening Standard*: he loves the urban, gossipy side of it just as much as yourself. Hey, you've got two red patches on your cheeks, he says, like a clown.

It's the cold, it's getting colder, can't you feel it?

How easily the lie slips out, it's stunning, so smooth, so quick. It's because your husband's trust in you is tethered like a buoy to a concrete block; you're the good wife, everyone knows that. Your palms fly to your cheeks to hide the heat and you look at Cole and think in that moment how easy it'd be to do anything you want, and, suddenly, how heartbreaking is his generosity and trust. You think, in that moment, that perhaps he never had an affair with Theo. It's so hard to imagine, as he sits in his shirtsleeves with his paper and olives and beer. You toy with the thought, for the very first time, that perhaps all along he was telling the truth. He never adequately defended himself from suspicion but maybe he couldn't: your mind was made up. Time is fading everything and you're beginning, suddenly, to doubt yourself: what you heard, what you decided upon so quickly. Perhaps, perhaps you were wrong.

That night you place your palm on Cole's chest as he sleeps beside you and you cup his heartbeat in your hand like a glass over a leech. You can't sleep, can't sleep. If you commit adultery in your head, are you beginning the rejection of your husband and your marriage and your life up to that point? Or welding yourself to them? And if that's the case, how does the marriage become, again, warm and rich?

Do you need an excuse?

You don't ever lie. Except to tell lovers that you've just had an orgasm or your friends that you love their new haircut and all of that doesn't count, it's done to soothe and protect. You don't steal. You don't sleep around. But you think about it. It's always been enough, just thinking about it, imagining sleeping with almost every man you meet.

What furious need is within you, you wonder.

Why must we crave the things we're not meant to, you wonder.

Lesson 51

Another Theo column. You're intrigued and repelled. You shouldn't read them, you know they'll just hurt; you can't stop.

As expected, there's something else about adultery. It's tucked into a query about a boyfriend who's unfaithful but gives great oral sex, and the reader wants him monogamous and every night, because it's all too delicious to pass up. And how can she have him all to herself?

> Dear Drowning in Deliciousness, the good news is that any man can be taught how to give great oral sex. Just curl his hand in yours and tell him to imagine the ridges are the folds of your flesh, and then demonstrate

with your tongue and breath and fingers exactly what you want. I guarantee it will work. But, dear Drowning, I'm afraid it's just not worth sticking with your boyfriend. How could you expect a committed relationship from someone who's been unfaithful in the past?

A committed relationship. Uh huh. What would she know about a committed relationship?

You crumple the magazine. Dare to tell Cole that Theo's column is rubbish, as is the whole paper that she writes for: perhaps this sentiment will be passed on. You wouldn't mind one bit if she knew she wasn't being read by you, that her wily messages weren't getting across.

Darling, I know the paper's rubbish, Cole says. I was only ever buying it for you.

Well, don't, you snap, I don't like it anymore.

OK. Whatever, Cole responds lightly and walks over, and opens his dressing gown and invites you in. It's an old gesture you've always loved. All your tension is released by it, your whole body relaxes into him.

Lesson 52

cheerfulness is a great charm in a
nurse

November flinches into winter and two red patches stain your cheeks, often now. Your heart catches in your throat every time Gabriel's voice is on the phone, your stomach churns and after the phone clicks in its cradle you run around the room and leap to the ceiling and bat the hand-made paper globes covering your lights and squeal to the sky. It's delicious and mortifying to be living like this again; so young, so gone. You never thought this belly-fluttering would ever come back into your life, that it would lie waiting for a waking no matter how old you got.

You have coffee with him. You go to the cinema at two P.M., theater matinees, National Theatre talks. He's gleeful that you have a car, wants to do London like a tourist; let's play in history, he says. You go to Kew Gardens and Alexandra Palace, Chiswick House and Hampton Court. He wants to drive; you let him. He's like a child with a toy, he's never owned a car. He takes you to his favorite space, the Rothko room in the Tate Modern, and after it you drag him to the Body section—come on, just a look!—and there's a Duchamp painting on glass and he watches your intrigue as you stand in front of the work: it's so odd, you can't make it out.

What, you ask, to his stare, go away, stop it, you laugh. Well, do *you* know what it's about?

Nope. And he walks away, laughing, his hands raised in abandon.

He's always leaping up for elderly men on the tube and engaging in chat with café staff and helping mothers with pushchairs down the steps. All the things you should do, but don't; all the things Cole would never contemplate. He's so compassionate, unhurried, relaxed. People aren't like that. It seems, almost, a naivety. How can he survive in the world? He's a man without scorn, and Cole, of course, is anything but. It's as if all the hardness that comes with living in London hasn't claimed him yet.

Sometimes, guiltily, you have afternoon tea in your flat and Gabriel takes out the rubbish at the end of it, without being asked, a small courtesy and yet enormous, for Cole always has to be nudged to do that. It felt so strange to have him in your space for the first time, you just watched: his lean, exotic darkness, his suit with his shirtsleeves poking out, his scuffed shoes with a piece of cardboard over a hole in the sole because, he said, Charlie Chaplin used to do it and it worked. He roamed the living room with his hands contentedly behind his back, peering at framed wedding photos and CDs and books; gathering evidence of how you lived your life. And how Cole did. He asked questions about him, as if he was endlessly curious about this marriage business.

Do you cook dinner for him?

Not much.

Do you ever wear an apron?

No.

He's enjoying this, he's smiling, his eyes are disappearing into slits: you love it when he smiles as completely as that.

Do you iron his shirts?

No.

Do you send him off in the morning with a peck on his cheek?

No. No. No, you shake your head, you laugh.

He opens doors for you, buys your tube ticket, pays the café bills, wouldn't think of anything else. It's days and days of small kindnesses, each with a tiny erotic charge, and they're returned all the time now—holding his hand, tugging him along, hugging him with delight—for the young child in you is skipping back. And sometimes there are no underpants under your knee-length skirt and this gives you a charge. It's just a small thing, for you, but enormous; unimaginable, a year ago. A private trespass, but no less arousing because of that.

Lesson 53

every womanly woman, who truly realizes
her mission, desires to be a pleasant object
of vision for her fellow creatures

Cole knows of him.

He'd insisted upon meeting the new library friends at one of the drinking sessions after work, he wanted to tag along. As if he just wanted to keep tabs on your new life; the price of the gift, perhaps. You had to say yes.

The actor one is creepy, he said, as you sat side by side on the tube on the way home.

Why?

He's in love with you, he said.

What makes you say that? Sweat shimmering across your brow like it does after too much chocolate.

I don't know, just a look, perhaps.

And Cole had returned to his *Standard*. Secure in his fiefdom, knowing implicitly the type of man you like and do not. He's always assuming he knows you so well: orders your drink without consultation, insists you try a particular dish he's sure you'll like, tapes you television shows he feels you should watch. And he always considers these gestures a kindness.

Gabriel never assumes, he wants to learn.

Two red patches on your cheeks, often now.

Your nails are painted for the first time in years and you keep on forgetting and catch in the corner of your eye the octopus fingers, it's as if they're weighed down with a life of their own. You write neater with them and eat neater and less. You're losing weight, there's a reason to now, and you've cut your hair short for you want people to see the new lightness in your face. You get contact lenses. You feel taller with them, bolder. You'd become lazy in so many ways, you'd stopped trying. You feel sleeker all over, walk with a subtle shine.

Your Elizabethan book takes on a new urgency as you dip into its pages:

> She decked her selfe bravely to allure the yes of all men that should see her. And who knows not how this deceipt of hers prospered and how much she is magnified and commended for the same.

You shut the volume, tremulously, you smooth your palm over its surface. You tuck the tiny book away in your drawer, suddenly not wanting Cole to see it lying around, to flip through the cocoa-colored subversion of its beautiful handwriting.

You're readying your life, but for what? You don't know where all the flirting and phone calls will end up. Does Gabriel feel the same as you? You don't dare to think ahead too much, for you don't want this melted under the heat of your attention, don't want it gone from your life.

Lesson 54

*H*ey, you whisper, poking your head over the wooden desk divider during a long library afternoon. I'm starving.

Go away, I have to work.

Come on.

He throws his pen at you, several heads look up, someone tuts. The café, you say, holding his arm with both hands and pulling tight.

Where are you up to?

The big scene. The bullfight. I have to get back.

Does the matador die?

Hardly ever now.

But I thought it was like Spanish roulette—someone always gets decked.

No, no, the sport's changed, there's not the tension that there used to be. The bull's no longer brave, and the matador's even less so. All the beauty in it is being lost.

The beauty in it, an erotic charge from that.

So, how *should* the bull die, you ask.

Like this, and Gabriel leans across the café table and caresses the back of your neck, he finds the vulnerable spot and whispers to you that that is where the dagger slides in, feel it, just there, it has to be clean, severing the spinal cord, he tells you there's a magnificence to the perfect thrust and as he speaks goose bumps sprint across your skin. You sit back. Rub your neck. You're shuddering for him, pressing your knees tight. There's an innocence to your face still, at thirty-six you could pass as twenty-six, as still needing to be taught, in your cropped cardigan and ballet slippers and knee-length skirt. The ribbons of muscle in your upper legs tighten, often now, at Sunday brunches with Cole's clients and dinner parties and in-law drinks; you're distracted by a want, achingly, for Gabriel to touch your cunt. *Cunt.* You've always hated that word and yet suddenly it arouses you; you smile, secretly, dirtily, when you say it in your head.

And yet you cannot imagine it ever coming to that for the one time you kissed—a cheek peck that strayed, a good-bye that went too far after a soaring afternoon—he jerked like a mustang being broken in. And whenever your skin brushes a touch he will retract, you can sense it, the pulling back.

Lesson 55

<u>at the end of the year you must see that your window box is tidy and in good order</u>

Darkness is greedy now, it crowds into the afternoons. The year is galloping toward Christmas. Cole's away a lot, networking at festive functions: drinks parties in creamy Belgravia drawing rooms and St James studios and private Soho clubs. For the first time since you've known him he hasn't asked you to accompany him. He recognizes, now, that he can't get you to do things quite so easily any more.

Gabriel's in Spain, with his extended family, he's not sure when he'll be back. He might do Prague afterward, and then Greece again, to visit a friend. You don't feel abandoned for you're secure in the knowledge that he'll return; the situation will resume exactly as it left off. There's a glamour to Gabriel's existence because he doesn't do the everyday. His contentment with few possessions is glamorous, and his lack of striving with his job, and his winging off constantly to some other place; it's all so brazen, flippant, audacious, light.

You tell yourself there's no crime in a cup of tea or a gallery visit or a skipping heart. You tell yourself your husband deserves your unfaithfulness because it keeps you with him, it keeps your marriage together, which is what you both want.

It will go no further. You don't want guilt like a sickness.

But during those long December nights you wonder why some people have a compulsion to allow chaos into their lives. To get attention? Sympathy? Love, to have it affirmed? Are you doing all this for Cole, perhaps; for him to notice you again, to be attentive, your best mate, like he was once?

Christmas is endured. Swiftly packed away.

I hate this between us, Cole says suddenly, on a very quiet New Year's night.

So do I.

Nothing else is said, it does not need to be said, there's just an unspoken acknowledgment that both of you want to slip back into an old way. The night is curiously healing even though nothing, still, has been sorted out. You're both in bed by ten. Cole wraps his warmth around you and you do not shrug him off. You cannot explain why your marriage works, now, but it does, enough. Enough not to have to set up your life somewhere else, to go back to the grind of City University, to rethink the baby plan. You've stopped asking Cole at every opportunity about Theo, the truth of what went on, for you've learnt that invading the mystery of each other's psyche will be more destructive to your marriage than a simple letting go ever is. So, you've let go. To reclaim your life. To navigate a way back into calm, if you can.

January. Cole has a job in Athens. It's for an old acquaintance who's in shipping, a billionaire who collects pre-Raphaelite nudes. But he's got something different this time, a portrait from the waist up of an exquisite medieval Venus and he doesn't want her out of his sight. Cole's shown you the photographs, he did the condition report, the paint is blistering and flaking off. There are several losses, patches of canvas totally bereft of paint, and Cole will have to take his palette and brushes and create a seamless match. He can't wait to get his hands on her. Her skin is pale and cold, as if it's been carved in marble. She has tiny buttons for nipples, like flesh-colored smarties, with no aureole, of course. There's a snake winding round her elongated neck with scales as soft and luxurious as black velvet.

Cole's gone for three weeks and your true self uncurls in this time. It makes you wish that throughout the years of knowing your husband you'd let him see more of who, exactly, you are. You can only bring her out when he isn't at home.

This.

The music up loud, *your* music, all the secret pop songs from your youth, Wuthering Heights and Blondie and the soundtrack from *Grease* and Nina Simone at her gravelly best, the type of music he hates, it's all crammed on compilation cassettes stored under the bed like a dietitian's secret chocolate box. You're dancing and singing off-key, too loud, drunk with the alone. You're rearranging furniture, dragging it in great grating shudders, how perfect you could make this space if it were just your own—out with that overlarge TV, off with the Scotch bottles and cheap detective novels! You're eating nothing but chocolate biscuits for dinner, a whole packet, or just a slice of toast and a glass of red wine and the dishes languish and the candles burn to their quick and at the end of each night you stretch on the couch and feel young and alive and sated and content. For alone you're refinding a glittering, a clarity, you're finding your distilled self.

You feel an intoxicating freedom when Cole is not with you, and yet you don't want him to be gone. You think of the two types of aloneness you've known recently: this wonderful, sparkly, soul-refreshing type, and the despairing loneliness that sucks the breath from your life.

Lesson 56

nothing impure should be left in a
bedroom one minute longer than is
necessary

A letter, heavy on the doormat. Thick,
creamy paper, watermarked, Italian, its edges feather-soft. A
sensuality to it you want to kiss. The words typed, the thud
of them as careful as braille.

*I want to remove your clothes in the darkness. I want
to unpeel you. I want to feel you, inch by inch.*

Your fingertips run over the words, deft as a lizard. You're
trembling, you cover the letter with your hand, you have to
sit with the strangeness of it.

I feel like you're helping me to live.

No name, no return address. Your dipping heart, seduced by text. You stand by the lounge room window with one hand holding the letter to your chest and the other spidered wide on the cold pane and your breath frosting the glass and your cheeks are hot. It's as if you're entering, tentatively, a strange new path and swiftly the trees are closing over you and the sky is gone and the light, you're lost, and in the thick of it, in a clearing, you'll be tugged down, drowned, in a bed of silk.

Come away. Start afresh.

The phone. Cole. All fired up. You know what's coming next: he'll be a couple of days late, he's still bent over that paint- ing, can't drag himself away. He's always loved telling you the minutiae of his work, you're a good listener.

You're looking at your watch and the letter as he speaks, wanting him off the phone. He's worried about his Venus's lips, some idiot somewhere along the line has had a go, clumsily, at touching them up and it's tricky to get them right.

Don't change them too much. No botox, mate.

Yeah, yeah, and he chuckles.

The point of his job is to work to a minimum, to do the least amount possible of fixing up because he's tampering with an original artwork. But sometimes, Cole's told you, he just wants to be let loose.

I want to cover her nipples, he says, she looks so cold. She needs some clothes, poor love.

Maybe she's blissfully happy, darling. Maybe there's a man under her skirt.

Oy, Cole laughs. Steady down. What's got into you?

Nothing, nothing, and you hang up the phone, grinning at the irony of a husband so absorbed in his job he hasn't seemed to have noticed the changes in his own wife's face over the past few months.

Lesson 57

do good and lend

*H*ow they've seduced:

Slow, enquiring fingers on your skin in an Edinburgh flat and you took off your pajamas as something flooded through you and you could not dam it.

Marijuana, once, but you fell asleep.

Alcohol. Champagne always worked best.

Porn. A video to soften you up and you were intrigued at first but the monotony quickly repelled and it was the coldest, most unimaginative fuck you'd ever had.

The urgency in a kiss.

An expensive hotel room that made you feel guilty.

A song that turns you on every time you hear it, a line in it: *she only comes when she's on top: crazeeeee.*

Compilation cassettes; and how many men have given you those? Why do they always think they know best? You'd never impose your own taste on them.

Letters. Letters have always worked.

But how would *you* seduce? How would you guard against scaring a man off?

They seem, often, so flighty, difficult, contrary, easily spooked. And you're not convinced that it's the men always chasing for in most of your experiences and your girlfriends' it's always the woman biting the bullet and doing the asking out, the hunting down. The looking, the not finding.

Lesson 58

you ought never to keep anything
whatever under a bed

Only Martha and you are left at the bar, for the library men have all gone home to their families, and after an awkward pause Martha asks if you've had a shag lately and you laugh and say no, not for ages, you've forgotten how to do it, it's been so long. Martha tells you she's slept on the couch for the last six years while her husband's in the bedroom, it's all very English, she tells you. We're high Catholic, we won't split. You laugh from deep in your belly, suddenly liking this woman very much. How seductive is honesty. You ask her, casually, about Gabriel, what she knows about him, you can't work him out. She looks at you sharply. Ah, Gabriel, she says, Gabriel, and she tells you she has a theory and leans close.

I don't think he's had much practice with women. He's probably only had one or two girlfriends in his life. I think he needs a bit of help.

What?

It's kind of exciting, don't you think?

God, I don't know, and you're knuckling your hands into your temples, you're thinking of the letter and the suits and the kind of man who wouldn't let a woman drive a car if he's in it, perhaps.

He's so . . . odd, Martha says. I mean, gorgeously so, but you know. There's something of the hermit about him, don't you reckon, the way he disappears for months on end and then suddenly turns up. God knows what he really does, or how he ever makes a buck. He doesn't open up to any of us. It's all just a bit strange.

You rub the line between your brow, trying to knead it out, and Martha laughs that everything's speculation, of course, and there's even vague talk of a girlfriend, once, who broke his heart but there's been no sighting of anyone since.

You know nothing of him. You've never even been to his flat. There's so much you've never asked. Deliberately, because you don't want to hear about a girlfriend in the wings, or a wife. It's better if you don't know, so that the spell is never broken; you're not ready for that.

But you feel a fatigue, now, at living within the web of your own tightly woven imaginings. Since a real man stumbled into it and began plucking at the silk.

Lesson 59

some use pillows stuffed with hops, but
the best preparation for sleep is honest
hard work and a good conscience

Cole's bags and coat crowd the hallway on
your return from a late morning trip to Tesco. He's home from
Athens a day early, without warning. Another letter's arrived
but he hasn't had a chance to sort through the mail and you
push the envelope deep into a pocket, listening but not listening to his travel chat.

The bathroom, as soon as you can. You sit on the toilet
seat, tear at the flap.

> Some days apart from you I'm in pain, my yearning is
> so strong. At times you settle over me like a great
> warmth. I catch myself smiling into space. I dream of
> us running away, getting out.

The fierce pull as you read, like a hand inside your stomach. The words so close you feel you could almost put out a hand. You touch the letter against your belly, feeling the smooth, cold paper against your skin. You get up, you've been too long, you kiss Cole absently on the crown of his head as he unpacks his bag and it plunges you back to a time when the love glowed, for a moment, and then it's gone. You sit at the kitchen table with the day's paper unread before you, your hands cradling your forehead.

Perhaps Gabriel is like Ruskin who, it's rumored, idolized women so much he was incapable of consummating his marriage when he discovered to his horror that his wife had pubic hair. Perhaps he's happily married in Spain, has seven kids; perhaps Martha's made it all up to throw you off the scent. Perhaps he's having an affair, is gay, caught by fear, can't bear to let anyone see who he really is. Perhaps he's one of those men who fell through the cracks—you know several, brothers and uncles of friends, lost men who've never found a sure footing with life, who are crushed by the challenge of living in this world and opt out and become loners or drunks. And put their parents, and lovers, through hell.

And then it hits.

What if he's never been with a woman.

What if he doesn't know how. A virgin, perhaps, and it all makes sense. The shyness. The pulling back at your touch. The ear tips blushing at a farewell kiss. Is it so implausible? You have an ex-colleague who's a virgin at thirty-two and you've never been sure about Rupert, your cousin. And he, like

Gabriel, is a tall, virile, masculine-looking man, and he, like Gabriel, never seems to be attached.

Would Gabriel be diminished in your eyes, if that were it?

No. It's oddly endearing. And exciting.

An idea, beautiful in its simplicity. To initiate Gabriel, to teach him exactly what you want. To create a pleasure man, purely that, the lover every woman dreams of. You'll be in control, for the very first time, you'll be able to dictate exactly what you want. And there'll be no expectation of how you should act.

That night Cole slips into your bed and curves his body in a question mark around your back.

An idea beautiful in its simplicity. And impossible.

For you don't do that type of thing. It's in the quietness of your clothes, your wholesome face, your ready blush. It's in your horror at hearing of affairs, your stock response: but I could never do that to another woman.

Or Cole. You don't think.

Lesson 60

A gift box is delivered. It's beautifully wrapped.

A vibrator.

You gasp. There's no note. It's obscene, fascinating, ridiculous, you've never seen one up close. You don't touch it for a long time and then you turn it round, sink back on the bed, turn it on. You can *control* it, make it go exactly where you want, for as long as you want, or as short.

It's small enough to keep in your handbag and your fingers brush it often, imagining exotic trips and Customs officers searching your luggage, having to explain it, stammering. You've never been searched, you've always been too innocent-looking and respectable for that.

There's no note with the package but the address label is typed. Your fingertips run over the letters, the heavy imprint of them.

Anonymous, of course. How long has he been back? Did he ever go? Is this another game? You ring, leave messages on his machine, he will not return your calls.

Another letter.

> I want to be the hand in the small of your back pushing you forward.

Trembling, wet, slumping back against the wall.
Snared.

Lesson 61

Another letter, until there are four. All typed, all short, and their words are etched like acid upon you.

Just to hold you, I ache for it, just to put my lips to the valley of your neck and slide down your body. I don't like being apart from you, not hearing your voice, not having you close.

The phone rings, five minutes after you've opened the last.

Heeeey. He draws out the word, he's always so playful with his greeting, as if it's such a lovely surprise to hear your voice.

Hey stranger, you respond.

I'm back, he says in a gleeful sing-song.

Since when?

Since right this second. When can we meet? Are you free?

Yes, yes, hang on, give me an hour, no two.

It's beginning to feel like infidelity as you get ready all stumbly and distracted, and the shower's too hard and too hot and you force your body into stillness with the slow warm ooze of red wine and then you close your eyes to some music, the Jeff Buckley CD Cole can't stand, *she tied you to her kitchen chair, she broke your throne and she cut your hair and from your lips she drew the hallelujah,* and you smile at the gathering wet, the expectation.

You walk tall out the door, alive, greedy, knowing. Possibility is wide open before you, as vast as a lake and you want to plunge in, dive deep.

No underpants.

Lesson 62

<u>the cold plunge: nothing can be more invigorating and delightful to a robust girl</u>

*H*e's already seated and you feel a tremor deep inside you at the sight of him, you're aching with tenderness as he sits in the café, across the street. He looks up and blooms a grin; your heart is filled up.

You run across to that greasy café with its beans on toast and stewed tea that's never hot enough, to where it all began eight months ago with a water splash. The letters are in your handbag and you're bold now, sure, and so thoroughly sick of all the uncertainty and tension, the games, the teasing, the waiting. You need to get this said, there are two red patches on your cheeks and you ask him straight out: why do we go on like this, we could, you know, just get a hotel room, or perhaps go back to your flat, or, I don't know, and you stop, you smile, so confident of his response.

His face.

Pardon, he asks.

His bewilderment.

Um, you hear yourself laughing, off-key, too much, OK, I'm sorry, and your face is stinging with embarrassment. But the letters you begin to say and then you stop and you snap: it doesn't matter. You excuse yourself, you have to go, you have to get out. You grab your bag, it's caught round the chair leg and you stumble out and walk down the street, bashing into shoulders and almost walking into posts and wait . . . wait . . . you hear behind you, but you don't turn back and at last there's the mouth of the tube station in which to disappear, to sink.

What have you done, what have you done?

Your head is in your hands on the tube hurtling home, knuckling your temples, trying to press it all out.

Fool, *fool*.

To think you knew him.

Lesson 63

*T*here's a light from under your front door. Your face is rearranged. Cole's cooked dinner, it's a mess, the water that was steaming the vegetables has boiled dry and the apartment's filled with the sour smell of a saucepan caked black. But he's tried.

A tight smile.

You haven't been writing me any letters, have you, the jittery blurt.

Letters, no. Why would I do that? What letters?

Oh nothing, nothing. I got a couple of letters. They were a bit strange. It might be this kid down the street.

What's going on? Is someone harassing you? Should we call the police?

God no, forget it. It's silly, harmless. What's to eat?

There's a Pandora's box of questions flying open in Cole's head, it is all in his face. You excuse yourself, can't force food down, feel sick. You've blundered from Gabriel, he's slipped from your life.

Fool, *fool*.

Is there something you want to tell me? Cole's voice is at the locked bathroom door.

No, no, forget it.

Let me see the letters. Who is this kid? There's concern in his voice, he will not let up.

I lent him some money for the bus and he's been on at me ever since. It's nothing, really, I can handle it. You manage a laugh. It's OK. All right? Your fingers twist your hair until it hurts.

OK, OK. A pause. Want a cuppa?

You wilt, you slam your eyes shut, you smile with your lips pressed tight.

Yes. Yes, thanks; your voice all choked. And then in the gap under the bathroom door a slim bar of Lindt chocolate appears. You can hardly voice your thank you. For at moments like these the charge in your marriage is suddenly, beautifully, back.

You succumb.

Lesson 64

<u>sweeping and dusting</u>

*B*ut not for long.

For the next day there's no call from Gabriel, or the next. Through late winter and early spring there's no contact, just an answering machine to receive your carefully rehearsed messages and he never returns your calls. The wind of agitation blows through all your nights, blowing away sleep until you fall, finally, into fitful technicolor dreams at dawn. Involving him, more often than not. He's wended his way into every corner of your life, he's a plasterer's fine residue, dust under a bed, a white film on a shower screen that keeps coming back and back no matter how furiously you wipe. You will him to surprise you, knowing in your heart he won't.

Just to hear his voice, so you can have your strength back.

You never imagined you had the capacity for such annihilation, never dreamt you could be reduced to something like this. The days stretch on, and the silence in the flat, and your nails are gnawed to the ragged quick and you draw blood chewing on your inner lips. You replay his bewilderment over and over in your head and exclaim out loud at the horror of it. It's like when your faculty boss years ago told you that his wife had just had a baby and how sad you'd replied, God knows why, how sad, and your strange, stupid words have haunted you ever since.

Why won't he call, to put your mind at rest? Did he never want to fuck you? Did he just want a friendship, do heterosexual male friends *ever* just want that? Was he stricken with embarrassment? Did he find himself falling for you and think it could never work? Your Elizabethan author's no help, she just ignites more questions, more doubt:

> *Witness the man who loved a woman so wretchedly and dishonestly that he could not be at rest until he defiled her; he forced her to lie with him, and afterwards, to make up the measure of his wickedness, he hated her more than he loved her before.*

Is it easier to just disappear?

The questions, the questions and the wind blows through all your nights, rattling the panes and whining to be let in. You toss and turn, as if you're vomiting sleep.

Lesson 65

poisons act in a way which are injuri-
ous to life

But then another letter, more beautiful, more
urgent than all the rest.

> *. . . You help me to live. You soak through the skin of
> my days, it's wonderful, torturous, transcendent all at
> once.*

Rubbing and rubbing at the line between your brow. Why
won't he just ring, why is he so opaque, does he always retreat? You're singed by the uncertainty, can't be strong in it by
yourself, you'll run from the mess of your world if you have
to and be alone, maddened, if you must.

There's no one to talk to, to ask advice. You want Theo's blunt opinion, miss the small pop when the cigarette is taken from her mouth and the talking begins, well, *this* is what you must do, girl. How many times has she said that in your past? She told you early in your relationship with Cole that she wasn't sure he was good enough for you; she said remember the Madonna song, don't settle for second-best, baby. But then she changed her tune when she saw over the years his kindness to you; she stopped her doubt after you told her that his capacity for tenderness always floored you and she was very still as you spoke: she had no answer to that. You wonder where she is now and what she's doing, as curious as an ex-lover and unhinged, hating yourself, lost.

You crawl on your knees in the kitchen, cramming your mouth with chocolate, block-sized bars of it and then biscuits, whole packets of sweetness, and ice cream and peanut butter from the jar, slurping it and sucking it from your fingers in great dollops of crunch, wanting to hurt hurt hurt and forgetting for an instant the power of slim. Unable to think, read, shop, write, to concentrate on anything very much for Gabriel invades all your actions and thoughts. All the efficiency and control of your professional self has been lost, and you're sleeping until all hours and then lying on the couch and staring into space, trashy gossip magazines unread on your lap. You can't bring yourself to ring any of your girlfriends, to see them for coffee or lunch, you're not ready to explain anything, can't. You don't want them judging your lank hair and spots, don't want their rallying or pity or fuss. You're phoning Gabriel and hanging up after two rings, you're phoning Theo and doing the same. You can hardly remember the woman you once were, the sensible university lecturer promptly awake, every morning, at six fifty-six.

Is it love, obsession, infatuation? You don't know. You think of a strange and beautiful word you read about once, Limerance, a psychological term, meaning an obsessive love, a state that's almost like a drug. Need like a wolf paces the perimeter of your world, back and forth, back and forth, never letting up. You're in a state that's focused entirely on the prey, and your fingers, often, are between your legs, stroking, teasing, stirring as Cole sleeps. You're appalled by the new appetites within you, kicking their feet and clawing to get out.

You find a calming, over the days, within the pages of your little book. The author's strong, singular voice never wavers, there's such a rigor to the text and its exquisite borders of red and black. Was she ever crawling on the floor over a man? You can't see it.

Maybe she never had a lover, maybe it was all in her head.

You wonder, suddenly, if she was unmarried, in a convent, perhaps; celibate, and so much stronger because of that.

Maybe her isolation was something she reveled in, for it enabled her to work.

Was the author contemptuous of the married state? Wanting to shake it up? Perhaps the book is even more subversive than you thought. You suspect she was writing it for any woman but herself.

> *Not woemen be in subjection to men but men to woemen.*

How had she been released?

Lesson 66

happiness and virtue alike lie in action
_____

_____

_____

May. The weather is unclenching, there's a lightness in the air.

The library stacks. The light's buoyant outside but gloomy inside. It's been a long time since you've come here. Each narrow passageway is illuminated by tugging a string at the end of it and your footsteps ring out on the cast-iron grates with the deadening clang of a jailer. A librarian returning books glances up from a floor below and you remember, too late, that you shouldn't be wearing a skirt in this place, it's an old Library lore: the wide spaces in the grates allow people to look up. To give you a shot of erotic courage you've not worn underpants but it feels suddenly wrong, you being here, in this state; trying to work but wondering if you'll see Gabriel by chance, trying to erase one obsession with another and in a place so soaked with them both.

He's not here. You just want to talk, to put your mind at rest. As you walk from the grills some of the grates shift slightly underfoot and the effect's dizzying and unpleasant and you're hating this ragged need in you that doesn't sit at all comfortably with your public face.

You sit at a desk. Grip its edge. Breathe deep. You have to concentrate on your own book, you must make it work: you need a spine to your life.

And then it comes to you, as beautifully and obediently as a tangle of necklaces that you've spent so long trying to unpick, and with the simple looping of one set of beads through another the knot of them magically comes apart.

You will respond to your mysterious seventeenth-century author.

You will write a book in secret, just like her. Why not? All writing is revenge, is it not. Yes, *yes*. You lick your lips. Reach for your notebook. And in an afternoon lost within the deep, deep peace of solid, consuming work, you produce three lists:

Men you have slept with, what you remember most.
How they seduced.
And on what.

Lesson 67

feather beds are a greater luxury than
mattresses but are said to be less
healthy

*B*eds, of course:

A stained futon on the floor. A sister's bed that smelt of grass. An attic eyrie mattress. A caravan bed that was vaguely damp. Your parents-in-laws' stern spare bed with sheets so slippery you fell off. A deliciously broad hotel bed in Hong Kong, wider than its length. Two single mattresses zipped together and you felt they'd break apart at any moment, they'd swallow you up.

And the non-beds:

A car bonnet. Shag-pile carpet that burned. A field of curious cows. A swimming pool at three in the morning, with the water buoying you under a circus tent of stars. There was the quiet as you fucked, you remember that so clearly, just the water's soft trickle and swish as you clung to each other and didn't speak, not a word, focusing on the intensity of the touch and the water's caress.

A hire car. Sand. A kitchen table at a maiden aunt's.

All the clichés. It's remarkable how similar most of the men's techniques were and yet how distinct each one is in your memory even if the name is not. You remember the unpleasant experiences more vividly than the pleasant ones; you remember why they didn't work. And your let-down. That it wasn't better than what you'd hoped, at the start, as your clothes were coming off. You always masked it.

It's a shame, that.

Lesson 68

<u>April is the hopeful month for garden-</u>
<u>ing</u>
_____

You visit the library again and again. You walk the bold iron skeleton of the beautiful building, *your* building as much as his. Just because he comes here doesn't mean you can't, and you slip off your shoes and arch your soles and your stockinged feet thrum on the iron. Strips of fluorescent tubing cast baubles of brightness here and there; above and below you readers sit or squat, isolated in their little circles of light. Old wooden desks wait at the ends of the passages like rest bays on a highway and there's the intoxicating smell of paper and leather, of words, waiting. You begin, finally, to tackle the book. To ask questions:

Why are women so constrained about pleasing themselves,

why are they so focused on everyone else's pleasure at the expense of their own?

What happens if they try to live selfishly?

But then a pool of light, philology, one vaulting spring day.

Your heart somersaults.

He is sitting on the ground with his back to a wall, reading and jotting on a notebook by his side. You do not go to him, you just look: his nape, his hair flopping into his eyes, his hand curled round the pen that clicks as agreeably as a lipstick, his watch from the forties with its broad, age-spotted face.

Something makes him glance up. He catches your eye.

His smile, like an umbrella whooshed inside out.

Yours back.

You're both trapped in this, you can see that. It's in his face.

Lesson 69

always say your prayers

A new café. He's holding your hand across the table, he's cupping it like a turtle's shell, he's not letting go; as if he's reluctant to abandon contact now it's been made. A cup of tea is in front of you, it's cold, a milky, spotty scum has tightened on its surface.

Gabriel, are you a virgin? Straight out.

Yes.

Just like that. You weren't expecting the confession so quickly. His smile has all the honesty of a desert sky in it; it's as if he's never uttered the affirmation to anyone and it's a relief, such a relief, to have it said. He says yes, again, yes, and his fingers are stroking yours absently, they're stroking your knuckles, they won't stop. And then he says I think I need some help, I've been thinking about this night and day and you're nodding, you're saying nothing of your own nights and days.

How come, you ask, soft.

He sits back, he laughs. Well, he says, slow, he's struggling to begin, he goes to say something, changes his mind. And then he starts. There was a girl when he was fifteen. Her name was Clare. They were in a musical together. It was a joint production with his boys' school in north London and the local convent school. He'd just moved there, from Spain.

What was the musical?

You don't want to know. *Salad Days*.

You both laugh.

She was American. Her parents were Spanish but she was from California. She was different from all the rest. Gorgeous. Warm. It was like, I don't know, she stored the sun under her skin or something. I was . . . gone.

You nod, you smile, it's a tale you can almost second-guess: that they fell in love, madly, sweetly, consumingly. That a teacher found them in a storeroom, during a rehearsal. That they hadn't got far but their clothes were off and you see the two of them: their hands, their faces, shy, shivery, wondrous, focused, scared. They were dragged apart. Clare's parents were very strict; she was withdrawn from the production; she never saw it. Gabriel was told not to phone, he wasn't allowed to see her, he sent a letter telling her he'd wait for her and he wouldn't look at anyone else but he never knew if she'd received it. She moved schools. He couldn't trace her, she was lost.

My family says I fixated on her, he says. I guess I did, I don't know. Not a single day went by without me thinking about her, and what I'd lost. Is that fixation?

I think so, yes, you smile. You turn your palm beneath his so that they're facing each other, flat.

Well, my mother says I have an addictive personality. He grins ruefully. Anyway, I was determined to be an actor—maybe, on some level, it was to find a way back to her, I don't know; I spent so much time pretending and imagining, it was all in my head. Anyway, one day when I was twenty I was walking down Charing Cross Road and she was just there, in front of me. He's nervous, there's a little cough through his talk, a clearing of his throat, you remember it from moments when he's been thrown off balance: when he has to query a waiter's bill, perhaps, or respond to a madman's belligerence on the tube. I'd been waiting for so long, he continues. We went back to my flat. Your hand tightens around his. Gabriel is silent, he licks his lip, he looks straight at you. I told her she'd have to be gentle, he says. I didn't know what to do. I'd never been with a woman. In my mind, I was still in the relationship with her. I'd been waiting so long.

You are holding his cheek, you are holding your breath.

She laughed. She just . . . laughed.

The anger in him still, after all these years.

She'd changed so much. There was such a hardness to her, she was so . . . cynical, knowing. All the sweetness was gone. And she'd dyed her hair and had too much lipstick, and this horrible, thick makeup on her face. She didn't need it, *any* of it. I don't know what happened to me. I grabbed her by the shoulders and I just shook her, I shook her as if I was trying to rattle the laugh out of her. I couldn't stop.

You press his hand between both of yours like a beautiful, smooth stone that you've found on the beach.

And then, I don't know, I lost focus, I couldn't concentrate, it was like some virus of insecurity was eating me up. Everyone knew me; girls, for God's sake, had posters of me on their walls; and as he talks he slips his hand from yours and his fingers worry at a paper napkin and begin tearing it into little holes. I couldn't say that I'd never actually slept with someone. I was paralyzed by it. I said to myself that by the time I was twenty-two I'd have been with a woman, and then it was twenty-five and then I was thirty and God, how could I tell anyone then? And weirdly, over the years it just became easy to say no. To pretend. It was like living behind a pane of glass and looking out at everyone, and not being able to touch. And he's laughing, soft. And then I met this woman, in a café.

Your breath catches in your throat.

I liked her, very much. He speaks so slowly; you can scarcely hear him over the hammering of your heart. And she was married, which meant, in a weird way, that she was free. There'd be no complications, no messy aftermath. I thought about it a lot. She was someone I could trust. And she was a teacher, too. It's funny, that.

Your mouth is sapped dry.

And yet I can't ask her to help me, it's impossible. I could never ask her that. She asked me once but I just blanked, freaked, I wasn't ready. And then . . . I couldn't face it. I'm sorry.

You look at him sitting before you, utterly naked, with such a helplessness on his face and his forehead all crinkled up and you're moved, so moved, by the courage of his honesty. You think of the contrast with Cole, the set of his jaw when you'd asked him again and again about Theo, the tightness in his hands as he'd pushed your questions away. Gabriel's making an enormous leap with his words, you're sure no one else has heard them. There was always a strange kind of absence to him, some piece of the puzzle you didn't have and now, suddenly, he is present, in such an endearing, transparent way and a tenderness is falling over you like a wave. You won't judge him or condemn him. In fact, you respect him; for not succumbing to all the pressure and panic about losing one's virginity, for resisting, holding out. It's so old-fashioned and disciplined, so austere, noble, quaint. No one does this any more.

Gabriel suddenly cringes and bows his head in his hands as if he can't believe what he's just confessed. This is a moment he will never forget in his life: tread softly, you must. Don't hurt him, don't scare him off, don't thicken that pane of glass. He's closer to you now than he's ever been, he's all vulnerable, stripped, and you know that you'll also remember this moment for the rest of your life, like a too-bright fluorescent light in a communal corridor that's never switched off, this moment of Gabriel sitting before you, naked, when all the nos that have been stopped up within you for so long become one enormous

yes.

Lesson 70

you had better have a millstone tied to
your neck and be thrown into the deepest pond than become a taker of opium

Walking to his flat. Not daring to talk; holding hands, tremoring, wet.

His rooms are spare and neat, like a monk's, with a
few beautiful objects from his travels here and there, and
small stacks of paperbacks and some black-and-white post-
cards on the walls. He does not intrude heavily upon the
space.

His bed's surprisingly big. You turn off the lights. Where to
begin, you are the teacher and before you is the blank slate:
God, the responsibility of it. You gather your thoughts, you

mustn't rush. You don't want him experiencing anything of the hurt or disappointment you've so often felt. How many women get the chance to do this, with a man, to break their virginity? It must be utterly memorable for him, something to savor for the rest of his life.

You tell him you want him to lick you, slowly, the inside of your wrist, and you push up your sleeve like a junky preparing for her first shot. Gabriel looks at you. He bends, hesitant. His tongue tip glides up your skin in one even, barely there line. Your eyes close, you let out a small gasp, his tongue stops. You take off his jacket, you unbutton his shirt, you find him, his vulnerability. His chest is cathedral-wide and your hands span its breadth like the vaults of a ceiling and you feel his galloping heart and you place your right palm over it, reading the race of it. He smells clean, pleasantly so, you can't catch anything of his real scent. His body is young, not quite finished, it feels strangely untouched, maybe it's the hesitancy in him, he's all caged up. Your lips walk the softness of his inner arm, slowly, daddy-long-legs-soft, climbing the paleness. You look up and smile reassurance and for some reason you hold his head like a mother with a child and he begins to say something and ssssh, you whisper, no talk and you hold his face in the clamp of your palms and he's concentrating so much, so intent, ssshh you whisper, ssshh, and kiss him slowly as if all the world's tenderness is gathered in that touch and as you do it your hands snake softly to the eroticism of his hips.

You kneel, unbuckle his belt.

His penis curves gently to one side, it's large; it always surprises you how big they can get. He is looking down at you, he is breathing fast.

You hold him, you lick him, soft, so silky soft, the tip.

He laughs nervously, he can't relax. He tries to push you off. You propel him, gently and firmly, on to his bed, on his back. Remove your clothes, quick; wet, so wet.

You sit, very slowly, on to him.

Ease down, slowly, feel him all the way. And then you just sit, for a moment, you are filled up and you smile into his eyes and very slowly you tighten your muscles and gather him inside you: you feel Gabriel with your skin. He looks at you, all wonder and surrender and shock, and you throw your head back, you can't look at him any more, you need to savor this moment alone. You keep on moving on him, slowly, rhythmically, with your eyes shut, ssh, you tell him, sssh, as he begins to say something, as you talk to him through your skin, you lean forward, you brush your fingertip on his lips, sssssh.

And then he comes.

He's appalled; it's so quick.

You smile, you stay sitting on him, feeling him in you, feeling him go soft. This, too, is delectable. Your hands fan upward on his belly and his chest, savoring his surprisingly soft skin, untouched for so long by any other woman and you bow your head and kiss him, in gratitude, on the cleft of his neck. You didn't orgasm, you didn't learn anything new but it's a start, a lovely one: for it's the very first time you've been totally in control. *Woemen bare rule over men.*

You climb off him. Stretch languidly, your palms turned to the sky as if they want to push it up. You feel like a cat on a favorite armchair it's never usually allowed on, thrumming with warmth and sunlight.

Gabriel rolls over on to his stomach. You walk across to him, lie beside him; your fingertips slip over each bump of his spine.

There *was* another time, he says, without looking at you. Your hand stops. It was my twenty-first, he says. I got drunk. My parents had thrown a big party for me. There was this girl, just some girl, a family friend, she was drunk, too, and we went up to a bedroom at the top of the house. But as I tried to go inside her I just . . . went limp. All I could hear was Clare's laughter. I couldn't go on.

You wing your arm across him, you squeeze his shoulder. Gabriel turns to you, he props his body on one side with his hand on his cheek.

So . . . thanks, he says, awkward, shy. Then there's a pause, and his impishness slipping back. What happens next?

You shake your head, you cover your eyes, you laugh: no, no no, we have to stop, all right?

Excuse me, madam, but you are not leaving this flat.

Lesson 71

those who eat too much should remember that they are robbing those who
have not enough

Walking by the river to the tube.

The Thames the color of cold milky tea.

Feeling intensely alive, as if years have been stripped from your body. Feeling engorged between your legs, plumped, softened, filled up. Smiling into the impatient dusk and flitting your fingers to your nose at the cocktail of smell, at the stamp of two bodies upon them.

Feeling as exhilarated as a teenager who's just finished the last of her exams, and the glorious stretch of the summer holiday is ahead of her.

———

But that night you're awake, vastly awake as Cole presses his trusting warmth into you. His hand rests on your hip and your eyes are owl-wide with this appetite for something else unleashed, it's all violent and terrible and exhilarating within you. Did Theo ever feel like this? Did she have guilt? Would she now happily resume her life? For you'd dreamt not so long ago of one transgression, just one, stemming the tide of marital disintegration and flushing you out, so you could begin, afresh, your married life; and never look back.

Your teeth nibble at a stubborn flap of skin on your lip, they nibble until there's a warm rush of blood in your mouth.

Lesson 72

*S*o it begins.

A weekday afternoon. Once a week. Always Gabriel's flat.

You're a good teacher, you always have been, and now after years of being the good teacher you don't want to just give, you want something back. There's one condition, you make it clear from the start: this arrangement must not, in any way, intrude upon your regular life. It's the only way you can make it work. When the lessons come to their end you will both disappear back into your worlds so that in the future, if you ever pass by chance on the street, you will not acknowledge each other or what you have done during these weekday afternoons in his flat. This will free you to explore exactly what you want. There'll be no photographs, no letters, nothing concrete about any of it, nothing to seize as proof. Memory is all that either of you will be allowed to keep. The rules come quickly and clearly, and make it easier to justify what you're doing.

Once a week. It's the only time you meet. For the rest of your waking hours you feast on the memory of what you've done.

The throb of that.

He opens the door in his suit, always, as if he's just come from work. The air in his flat smells of inner London, of too much traffic standing still and the taste of iron is in your mouth. Business people walk by his ground-floor window, chatting on their mobiles, in their clattering heels and brisk shoes. It makes the lessons seem more willful, childish, indulgent, like a sunny afternoon stolen from work, spent, secretly, at a film. But worse, much worse.

So, week by week. Slowly, you do not hurry. You feel you have all the time in the world to savor each other, having rushed in with that first, miraculous fuck: it was just a start. There's so much to learn, now. For both of you, for as you teach him you'll be teaching yourself although he doesn't have to know that.

A rough agenda is set.

One, the removal of clothes. You learn his skin, inch by inch. He, yours.

Two, the touching, the licking. Exactly where you want. The

lobe of your ear, the tip of his tongue on your upper mouth. The skin below the vagina, its tender rim, your clit. You tell him exactly where you want him, you guide him, instructing him to slow down or not stop or don't move or stay on track. And with that, finally, as he listens intently and does precisely what you want you have your first orgasm and a whole new world is opened up: your eyes are clenched with the warm flooding wet and you scissor on the bed and arch your back, trying to squeeze the last shudders out or prolong them, you know not what, and still the implosions shoot through your belly and then soften and stop, and you can't move, you're drained, all you can do is lie on the bed and laugh, in shock. Gabriel looks at you. My God, he says, my God he repeats. You sit up. Run your hands through your hair. You have to concentrate: this can't be just about your pleasure, it's Gabriel's turn. With him giving you so much you want to present him with a flooding of delight back: you have a goal, for the very first time in your life, to see a man completely laid waste.

By your hands, lips, tongue. If you can.

So, the licking, where *he* wants: most of all, the flattened front of the tip of his cock and then its underside, he can hardly bear your mouth on it and yet can't get it enough and while you're doing it you squeeze the base of him tight. You discover it all together, you're both learning so much and you look up, to his eyes: astounded, delighted, both of you. Then the rim of his asshole. His balls, the firmness beneath and it's his turn to tell you not to stop.

Three, the clandestine public kiss, fully clothed. The bedroom kiss, unclothed, the places for it.

Four, a candlestick. The handle of a hairbrush. The neck of a champagne bottle, and how thrillingly gentle you both have to be. Why is it that inanimate objects can excite you more than a penis ever does?

Five, the vibrator. Teasing your clit and hard in you. Under the head of his cock and in his ass and you savor the clench in his face as he comes.

Six, porn magazines. He has to buy them, it's his task. You want the letters pages, nothing else; you're not interested in what he does with the rest. You revel in saying all the words that've never slipped comfortably from your tongue: *cunt, fuck, ass*. You're the housewife with the angel face and a sudden grit in her talk and it's as if your outside and insides no longer match. Fuck me, you tell him, come on, fuck my cunt and you're appalled and aroused by the words slipping from your mouth.

Seven, wrists bound to the bed posts. Disabled, blindfolded, tied up.

Eight, the shower, rammed against the tiles.

Nine, sleep. Curled around his back, your body his blanket, your palm on his heart because sometimes, you tell him, that's all a woman wants.

Ten, the fuck. The first time didn't count, there was nothing to be learnt, it just had to be done. You need time for it now, to get it right; you're determined, finally, to make it work. He's too jerky, grating, mechanical, you knew it would be like this, there's no music to what he's doing and he comes too quickly, of course. You'd always wanted it quick with Cole; but this is different, you have to find the exquisiteness you know exists. You'd been hoping for something different with Gabriel but the fucking, for you, is still not catching alight. You make a heroic effort not to show him your disappointment, not to turn away in frustration, sulk.

You take a deep breath.

Tell him, gently, that you both need some practice at this. Tell him he needs to slow down a little, look at you, not lock himself into his own little world. Tell him you're not, actually, getting a thing out it. He snaps his head away from you, he's so annoyed, feels he's come so far, it's hard to tell him it's just not far enough. He gets off you. Leaves a sticky mess. You grab at him, tenderly, in apology, but he storms to the bathroom and tells you he's had enough.

You don't contact him for a week.

Ring the morning of the next session and he answers, too quick.

Can I see you this afternoon?

Yes: grumpy, abrupt.

Good, you say, I'm so glad, you say, warmly, knowing this would be his response. And wanting him so much.

Gradually, gradually, you slow Gabriel down, allowing him in a fraction at a time, pulling away if he tries to rush. Teaching him that a key to the exquisiteness lies in the waiting, the refraining, the holding back; and you've both been experts at that, ever since your hands brushed a touching in a café as a phone number was handed across. You tap into that now: enforcing the rules of no contact during the week, not removing your clothes the instant you walk through his door, sitting down over a cup of tea and then slowly, absently lifting up your skirt, no underpants, of course, and lightly touching yourself as you chat. Widening your legs, flexing your back, watching his distraction, his inability to stay seated: gathering his head to your kiss as you come.

You get Gabriel to feel you as if he's a blind man reading the secrets of your inner skin. You make him vary his rhythm, gently admonish if it strays into monotony, teach him the secrets of tenderness, relaxing, surprise, teach him everything that you want. You iron him out until your inner thighs are fluttering and your pelvis is aching from stretching under him, until your thighs are trembling hours after you leave and into the next day.

Gabriel wants the lessons more frequently than you, he rages against the pleasure he's missed, he's afraid of time running out. It's as if he wants to make love incessantly to cement what you're doing in his life, to make your time together solid and settled and a habit you both cannot break. He says he is happy, so happy. He never thought he could have such greed in him.

You hold him, you laugh, squeeze him tight. You don't tell him you feel that too.

You will not be hurried. You refuse to increase the frequency, to quicken your pace: you want to linger. You will not lengthen the lessons into the evenings, despite his insistence. When the dark comes you must stop. The lessons can only be conducted in the light, it's like you're living in fear of falling asleep with Gabriel and being kissed awake in the morning light, and being trapped, forever, in his life.

It's as if you've never felt pleasure until now. It's as if what passed as pleasure before was a cardboard cut-out of it. For you've never been in control, until now; you've never, before, had exactly what you want.

Lesson 73

You want Gabriel's finger in your ass as he's fucking you, you tell him that, you've always wanted to try. There are so many things you've always wondered about and now there's a willing partner who'll never embarrass you, for he'll never be entwined in your normal life. With his finger in your ass you have your first orgasm while a man is in you and you smile wide, you can't stop: you could grow to love this too much.

And then the licking, whole golden afternoons of it. It's never quite worked for you: Cole, particularly, always thinks he knows best. Now you tell Gabriel exactly where you want him, around the clit most of all and you splay your fingers on each side of it, you straighten them to draw back the flesh. It stands bold, a wild red. You lift your lower back and press his mouth on to you and you won't let him come up as you twist your fist into the sheet. And then he breathes you in gently and his tongue dips into you, it sweeps deeper and deeper and you didn't know you could ever get so wet. He stares at you as you come, stares at what he's done and you turn your face and tell him not to look, go away; you don't want him to see you so cracked apart. But he keeps looking, gleefully, his fingers held over a smile, as if in prayer.

But I love you like this, he says. I just love it.

Gabriel's not afraid of your sexuality. Your pleasure is giving him pleasure, it arouses him and he asks nothing physically of you in return: no one has taught him to do that, to expect. He's your first lover who's utterly selfless, there's no request to go down on him, it's purely unselfish, feminine sex.

Your orgasms are becoming increasingly intense, they trip over each other until almost as soon as his tongue touches your skin you have to push him away and thrust your fingers between your legs, trying to stem the coming, to slow it down, and you slam your face into the pillow, muffling sounds you've never uttered before that break from the base of your spine.

You feel so alive. Shaken awake after years of apathy until you're almost coming with just his kiss in greeting, or the sound of his voice on the phone.

You wonder sometimes if he enjoys the licking that much, for a colleague let slip once that the taste of a woman, when he went down on her, always made him gag, that there was no woman whose smell he'd ever liked even though every woman's smell was different. But you're addicted now and many afternoons he'll be between your legs until your inner thighs are trembling and you're begging him to stop for it's too exquisite, it verges into pain now, you can hardly bear it. And yet he goes on, as if he's trying to stamp out the memory of any other man's fuck and you're drowning in the pleasure of it, you're glutted, keeling, lost.

You kiss, softly, the valley at the base of his neck, you kiss, softly, the pale clearing behind his ear, you breathe him in deep, kneel, swell him. Want to give so much back, to have him as stunned by sensation as you are.

Changed, utterly.

And each week hurtling home on the tube you wonder where it can all end, how much more can you ask of him. For everything else is obliterated by that explosive pleasure at the base of your spine, your whole other life is wiped away. Neither of you talks about husbands or families, or what on earth comes next, because you can't bear to think about anything that might put a stop to all this.

Lesson 74

<u>go to bed not later than ten and get
up at five or six when you are grown-
up</u>

You ring your mother. It's her birthday;
you've sent some lovely, hand-made Spanish riding boots that
were way too much but you feel so generous and large-spirited
in this new life.

Hey, you sound great, she says.

Yeah, I feel it. I'm getting lots of rest, and exercise.

You want to tell her about Gabriel, burstingly, but if anyone finds out you'll have lost a little of your control: you'll
never know when it could slap you hard in the face.

Keep doing what you're doing, she says in farewell. It's
working, darling.

You smile. Take down an old photo from the mantelpiece.
Your mother's in the Gobi Desert, on a dig site, a bucket in

one hand and a spade in the other, and her eyes are narrowed against the sun and strands of hair whip across her face. You used to hate her loose, loud life when you were growing up: the way she'd wander around the house naked, push you out to experience something of the world, take you to interminable dinners to meet yet another of her men.

You recognize now that your mother was doing exactly what she wanted and, in her mid-fifties, she's still doing it. She's now contentedly celibate. Living a vivid life, which sometimes involves watching old black-and-white films until three A.M. and sleeping until midday and having just tea for breakfast and nothing else. Jumping on a plane at the news of a fossil find, gone for a month. Reluctant to go on dates. Shying away from what they might lead to: some sort of sharing of her life.

They're so boring, the lot of them, she says. All they want to do is talk about themselves. Or stand you up. I'd much rather go out with a girlfriend than a man.

Most of her friends are divorced, don't want another man, seem happier by themselves. They've done the kids, they've been the good wife. But you wonder if your mother's being completely honest with you. Who really chooses to be alone? So much energy, in your adulthood, has been spent trying to escape from that state.

You wonder what your mother would make of you now, with your secret life. If she'd approve; if she'd worry for Cole or say it's the best thing for you both. He's been so buried in his work that he doesn't seem to have noticed the languorous fullness of your movements as you prepare his dinner. Hasn't noticed your fingers savoring your swollen, reddened lips as he watches television, chats, eats.

You're a good wife, a good actress: it's surprisingly easy, the cover-up. You were acting all along and scarcely realizing it. But you want to grow old with Cole, you still want that. You'd be perfectly happy never to have sex with your husband again, except to create a child; and you've heard that before from married friends. Cole represents something larger than sex: he's embedded in your life plan.

But where does desire go? Will this fugitive feeling eventually die out? Or now that it's loosened will it lurk within you into old age, all rangy and discontented, just waiting to trip up your life?

You've been careful, Cole will never find out. Gabriel won't tell, for you've been entrusted with a secret about him that virtually guarantees that. How mutually beneficial it all is, how perfect: you've found a lover who'll do exactly what you want.

Who'll never talk.

Who's woken you up.

Lesson 75

<u>the shoddy trade</u>

A gift box, just like the one that held your vibrator. It's beautifully wrapped. Handcuffs. No note. You smile, you don't need to ask anyone now.

They lead to a new lesson, with the bedhead. There are the sharp, hot spurts of your cum; it's such a lovely shock. Your voice is deepening when Gabriel's in you, it's dropping an octave and you listen, astounded, to the woman you're becoming.

To be fucked in the ass, something you've always wondered about. The pain, the exquisiteness, the *illicitness* of it. You don't want it often, it has to keep its edge, you need it to remain unique.

Gabriel wants it a lot, but he respects your wishes when you say no, he backs off.

There's a beauty to his carefulness, his intent; you think, with some amusement, that he learns with the focus of a first-time driver who's never before sat behind the wheel. He's so earnest and grateful. You teach him to touch with assurance, confidence; you teach him to mask his fear, but you can tell that love, for him, will be a vice when it comes, will grip him hard, will swallow him complete. Your heart already bleeds for him, for what is ahead.

He's still glamorous to you; his honesty has glamour. You love his chuff when you come, you love watching his eyes, delighted and astounded, at you as much as himself. You can't bring yourself to tell him that so much of this is new for you, too, that in some ways you began these lessons as virginal as he. That everything you want has been, for so long, in your head; that you've never spoken out.

Your Elizabethan woman did, it's in the confidence of her voice. You hear her whispering, delightedly, through your blood: go deeper, further, don't slip back.

There are many women admired not so much for their virtuaes, as for their vices and imperfections.

Lesson 76

<u>few women pass through life without being called upon to nurse a relation or friend</u>

Your mother rings. Theo has called.

Really? Why?

I don't know. She just wanted a chat. She remembered it was my birthday.

I haven't spoken to her for a while.

She said that.

We had a bit of a falling out.

She said that, too. What was it about?

Oh, things. I just felt that she was crowding me. I was beginning to feel a bit suffocated by her.

It's not such a bad thing, perhaps. People come and go. I always thought she was so high-maintenance. Exhausting, you know that.

Your mother's reservations about Theo used always to be the flint for another fight but you see it now, she's right. Your best friend was vastly entertaining but the flip side was the constant calling, the jealousy at any new lover or friend and, most smothering of all, the insistent interventions in your own life. Your mother had categorized Theo as overwhelming from the age of thirteen: she'd requested you be placed in separate classes at the start of the next term and out of fury at her meddling you didn't speak to her for a month.

She said that Tomas and her are trying for a baby, she says now, as the conversation winds down.

Oh?

She wanted you to know.

Oh.

So, Theo gets in first. She always does, from starting her period at eleven to losing her virginity at eighteen to getting married: and now this. Why has she chosen to keep you informed, does she want you to know that something has passed?

You hadn't told your mother about Cole and her; dreading the knowing in her voice, perhaps, wanting to sort it all out for yourself. Now, it doesn't seem worth letting her know. You're moving beyond it. The rage is softening from you, at last; like a fire collapsing into its embers, it's almost out.

Lesson 77

rules for choosing

As autumn encroaches upon the light, sometimes there's just sleep with Gabriel, nothing else, several hours of it; skin to skin and his lovely warmth. And as you lie there you think of the next step, perhaps: groups of men, anonymous sex, women.

You think, where does this stop?

You can't imagine how you'll end these afternoons but some day you must. You fear, already, they're slipping into something else, you can feel a binding being spun over you both. On the first day of November Gabriel washes your hair in the bath and then you his, and afterward you hold him so tenderly, so quiet, and you wonder at all that has happened over the past few months, a summer so different from the last.

You've made love like you've never loved before, you never felt capable of such giving, or such a response. During the sex with Gabriel you've grown younger, you've utterly let go, you've showed another person, for the first time in your life, your true self. A woman who astounds you and scares you. A woman demanding, selfish, sparky, in control. He's made you feel accomplished as a lover, he's given you confidence.

So, it has come to this, and neither of you will speak out about what comes next. On the tube hurtling home you think of those sounds breaking from you that you've never uttered before, and the arch of your back, and your fist clutching the sheet. But then you're home, promptly, by six, you're never late. And every night there's Cole pressed into you—his arm, or the cheek of his bottom, or the length of his torso—every night there's his exhausted, trusting weight. You prize your husband still, so much: you don't want all that he represents gone from your life. You lie awake trying to find a way for your needs and your wants to coexist peacefully; you don't see, yet, how they can.

Yes, you did begin, with Cole's gift of freedom, you did find a way to fill up your days. You're living with the light and the guilt of that.

It's a seesaw of delight, and doubt.

3

As it has been said:
Love and a cough
cannot be concealed.
Even a small cough.
Even a small love.

—ANNE SEXTON

Lesson 78

when a girl has a rosy, healthy face we
know that her lungs do their work well

---

*T*he more sex you have, the more you
want.

Perhaps, now, a man who's always insisted on doing it his
way, which you haven't liked enough. You sit at your desk,
with your thumbnails hooked between your teeth, and smile
at the challenge of that.

A Saturday afternoon. You tell Cole you're stuck with the
book. You laugh that you might end up throwing it all away
and having a bit of fun; you might just write about what
your Elizabethan housewife was really interested in—sex.

You?

You flick suds from the dish-washing brush. Yes, me. Maybe I'll write about what women really want, mate.

Oooooh, he says, holding up his hands in mock terror.

Half an hour later, languid with laziness. Lemony sun through the tall windows, dust motes dancing in the light. The magazine supplements of the weekend newspapers are scattered across the bed and Cole comes into the room and he kisses you on the lips, in his special way, and he says, so what *do* you really want, and there's a new intent: it's as if he's finally responding to the new energy that crackles around you and you do not shy away from his kiss. You whisper to him you want him to shave you; you've never said anything like that to him before.

His sharp, soft intake of breath.

His voice is barely audible, one word, yes, just. He looks at you as if he always suspected there was a woman like this underneath. He goes to the bathroom and retrieves your razor, and changes his mind and brings out his own: it's sharper, he says, more effective, excitement in his voice and that strange new intent, and you lie on the bed with your thighs spread wide and outside is the buoyant sky, the air fat with the coming summer, and you don't know what to expect. You wait for Cole with one hand between your legs and the other thrown above your head. Your nipples are erect, they've rarely been hard for him over the past few years, as if they couldn't be bothered getting into that state. Now you want him, quick: you're already arching your lower back, in soft waves.

What's got into you, he asks.

You say nothing, your hand hooks him behind his neck and pulls him down to a kiss. And then he begins, and as he's brushing his razor through your pubic hair a change plumes through you like ink shot into water, you start to feel young again, a teenager, to feel with all the intensity of those years. Something's combusting within you, it's like a varnisher's hand whipped over a painting, as if all the leaden textures that have dulled your life for so long are shot through with light. You open your mouth and gulp air, you bunch Cole's fingers in yours and squeeze them tight. At the end of it you both stare in fascination and horror at the childlike slash. Cole scrabbles off his trousers as if he doesn't want to lose the moment, as if he, too, knows how rare it is. He comes quickly—too quickly, he thinks—but for you it's perfect and you turn from him to the windows, to that lovely lemony light, and smile a Cheshire smile.

For you've just had your first orgasm with your husband.

Later that night. An Italian restaurant round the corner, your favorite. You haven't been there with Cole for ages; you used to go often when the relationship was young. What's got into you, he asks again, over a bottle of red that's spreading warmth through you both. You smile, your hand hovers at your throat.

I've found this special section in the library, you say, it's full of these books, erotic books, and you stop, you blush, you cannot go on.

Cole leans back in his seat. He folds his arms like a headmaster who's just heard a fantastical tale of remorse.

I keep on going back to them, you say.

Well, here's to the London Library, then, and he raises his glass.

Lesson 79

<u>no dirt should be left in the interior</u>
<u>crevices</u>

You don't tell Gabriel, you let him discover
for himself. You're not wearing underpants, of course. You feel
an exquisite vertigo as he kneels before you, as his hands push
up your skirt.

He recoils.

What's this?

Cole did it.

Gabriel tightens, his whole body, his face.

Are you still sleeping with him, he asks.

Well, yes. He's my husband.

There's a prickle of irritation at having to say that.

He gets up and goes to the bathroom. The door slams
shut.

Gab? Gabriel?

He talks through the door: I just didn't think you were still fucking him. I thought—and there's a sigh.

What? Gabriel?

I don't know. I don't know what I thought.

I'm married, remember.

Gabriel comes out, he is flushed, he sits you on the bed and his hands hold your upper arms. He says that you're unhappy with your husband, you've been unhappy with him for so long, he asks why you're turning back to a man you don't love. I never said that, you bristle, you shake your head: it's too big a question, he has no right. He says let's go to Spain, let's go be together for more than a few hours.

There's a little villa by the sea, that my family owns.

You stand. You know in this moment that Gabriel is at your mercy, you can do what you want, he is completely yours and with the knowledge of that something goes, you can feel it slip from you like a fish through the net.

I don't want this to stop, he says. You don't either, he says. We can't. We're part of each other's lives now. You *know* it. Don't lie to yourself. I feel like the past couple of months have been the happiest time of my life; the only time I've been living.

You step back. Gabriel has fallen in love and you almost despise him for it; it's all messy before you, he's a man wild with uncertainty and want. He's broken the rules; insisting on exclusivity and demanding nights. You're not sure, suddenly, what it was that bound you to him. Infatuation, perhaps. The craving for a man to be tender with, to touch. The challenge, the thrill of the chase. Revenge. The desire to learn, to open up your life.

And then he was caught.

And you're at a loss, in this moment, over what to do next.

You stand before Gabriel with your hand covering your mouth, as if in shock at some terrible news, as if you're about to be sick. You feel you're learning everything about love as you watch him, from the other side. He imagines you leaving your cozy London world for a man in his thirties who has no real job, who still travels on buses, who's never found a firm footing with his life. The poet, the dreamer, and you would have fallen for it once. But you're too old, now. You just want to fuck. As did the author of your little book.

> *Where trow yee finde a man be hee ever so kind and curteouse to his wife that was willing to substitute an-other man in his place.*

There was nothing in there about leaving her husband. That wasn't the point.

Gabriel's still on the bed, the heel of his fist at his fore-head. You assess with your head, not your heart. You want him to have more of a life than you, to have other women, to open out his world. The idea had once given you a frivolous thrill: you dreamt of him going off and finding other women and learning their secrets too, and bringing all that he gathered back to you.

Like a snail prodded with a stick, you retreat.

Are you going home to your husband, he asks.

Yes.

Fuck you.

There's such a force in that "fuck you," it brings you up sharp, it's a side of him that takes you by surprise: he's masked it well.

And fuck him too, he spits.

Something curdles up within you; a defensiveness, a protectiveness. Leave Cole out of this, you say. You want your husband, suddenly, very much. His calm, his dependability, quiet. You fear for him suddenly, for what Gabriel might do. For you've seen now the vehemence of someone who shakes a girl to rattle the laughter from her, shakes her so hard that she will never come back.

You dress. You leave. In silence.

Lesson 80

opium eaters grow lean and hollow-eyed
and yellow-skinned, and always appear
to be looking out for something

The lessons must stop. You can see Gabriel, suddenly, hijacking your life.

And you have a strange, new tugging in you for Cole; you weren't expecting it, you never thought the moribund relationship could be woken up.

You stick out your arm for a cab and feel the vivid bareness between your legs as you stretch your body out. The cab driver asks you where you want to go, he's young, not very good-looking, a father, perhaps. But he has a beautiful nape. You say, bewildered, barely thinking, I want to have sex, do you want to sleep with me, I need it, please, and he turns and looks at you, he pulls up. You repeat the question. You will never see him again, you will make sure of that. You will dye your hair after this, you will change your look, you will be someone else. You say, I'll meet you in two hours at . . . at . . . and across the street, a little way up, is a Hilton Hotel. At the Hilton, you say. The room will be under Green. And you are floating as conventions and assumptions drop away on all sides and the words slip from you, so easily, so quick, for you've rehearsed what to say, what to do, for so long, at night, in your head.

Two of you would be good, you add, I think.

He looks at you, as if he knows exactly where you're coming from. You turn your head, your fingertips appalled, trembling, at your mouth. He lets you out. You pay with a twenty. You do not take the change. He doesn't say if he will come.

You know exactly what to do. You ask at a paper shop where the nearest hole in the wall is. You get out cash, a lot. You check in under the name Green, you like the name Green; you give Theo's address. You hand across your credit card for an imprint, realize suddenly it has your surname on it but the woman doesn't even check, you're too respectable-looking for that. You go to the room, you shower, you pour yourself a glass of red wine, and another, and you wait.

There are three of them.

You tell them to do anything.

Your face is still young, still sweet, you can see their surprise: they never expected this. It is what you have always wanted, even as a child on the cusp of adolescence, you'd always dreamt of it, naked, spread-eagled, and a group of men or boys fondling you, curious, growing bolder, getting more excited, moving in. You do the things you've always wanted to do, what you devoured in the letters pages of the porn magazines you filched from your uncle when you were fifteen. You are not shy with these men because you are not interested in any connection being made, you're not interested in talk, in anything that will give you away. You will never see them again. You will not be coming to Gabriel's flat anymore, the lessons must stop, you will not be getting a taxi for a very long time. This will be the end of this chapter in your life. It is all worked out and so you are free, in this hotel room, to do whatever you want.

They are rough, whether they sense that is what you wanted or not you don't know. It is what you want. They don't respect you. You are nothing but a vessel, a series of holes to be filled up. Your cunt, ass, mouth, all are used, sometimes simultaneously, all are fucked. You are passive, compliant, it is exactly what you want. To erase Gabriel, to start afresh.

You tell them when you've had enough, they're reluctant, you push them off. *Go*, please, get out.

You don't want a shower. You catch the tube home, your head bowed, you are reeling, triumphant, your palms cupped across your mouth and nose. Breathing in deep that afternoon that you will never have again, that you will never forget, while the stiffness in your thighs sets. You are engorged, swollen, and a trickle of cum leaks from you as you shift on the seat, you can feel it, and the rawness between your legs, and on your pubis, from the stubble of the men, it burns, the harsh grate, God knows how long it will last.

You're home, promptly, by six, you're never late.

Grubby and aching, and exhilarated and cleansed, re-freshed.

Lesson 81

take a warm bath, put the feet in hot
water and mustard, take gruel and then
go to bed well covered in order that we
may perspire freely

*B*ut it doesn't wipe him out.

You think of Gabriel deep into that hurting night, your hand between your legs, balming the ache, trying to press it out. It felt like he was pushing you deeper and deeper into life and it was all brought so suddenly to a halt: because he said that the rules should no longer exist. Why did he have to destroy the secret world you'd created for each other? He smashed it with love, with attachment. There's no returning now, for God knows where it would end up if you did.

You imagine Gabriel waiting for the call that will not come. You've waited so many times in the past; a hostage to a lover's silence and you know too well the heart-slam of what

233

it's like. You're tinkering so thoughtlessly with his life and not cleaning up the mess. You've created a woman's dream lover who knows something of the secrets of what women really want, and what they don't. But what *do* women really want?

You're not sure, now.

A cherishing? Money? Security?

They don't, necessarily, want to fall in love.

Cole lies with his back to you and the arch of your foot locks into the warm curve of his calf; you often do this as he sleeps.

Lesson 82

never sit in a thorough draft

The phone rings the next day and the next, Gabriel's usual time, and his voice is on the answering machine but you do not pick it up. After the call on day three, at the same time, you slam the door shut on the flat.

You want the taxi drivers again. They take their breaks in the green cabby's hut by Notting Hill Gate. The Scottish one told you that, the one with the face that looked as if it had been scrubbed raw by the wind, he told you he wanted you every day inside the hut, as he shoved his prick into your aching, numbing cunt; he said that he'd boot the dinner lady out. He wanted all his mates there too, he said, as he flipped you over, he wanted you spread on the table, he said, as he was fucking you up the ass.

You sit at the bus stop opposite the green hut. You're perched, uncomfortably, on the red plastic bar. You will wait it out. It takes one and a half hours. The first driver you spoke to pulls up and you walk to his window. You don't say anything. He looks at you, he grins, he slides his window down.

I want a woman as well, you say.

He sucks in his breath, you can see his savoring but he doesn't want to let it out. Uh huh, he says. I'll need a bit of time, he says. Let's make it six o'clock.

You go to a public phone box. Tell Cole you'll be home late. Martha's had a trauma, she needs to go out and have a drink, talk it through. You walk from the box, thinking of being licked by a woman while the men watch; of being urinated on, of being filled up.

You wear just a bathrobe as you open the hotel room door. You don't want them to see your clothes, to read you in any way, you don't even want to give them your voice.

Two men this time, and a woman. As soon as you see her, it's wrong. She's young, wary, a friend not a partner, in it for a laugh. She wears a white shirt that's grubby round the collar and you're annoyed by that. She's assessing you, reading you, she knows you in a way the men never will. It's suddenly shameful. You lie down, awkwardly, on the bed. The sheets are too slippery. You feel cold. You can hear the television news too loud in the next room. Nothing works, it's utterly unerotic, it hurts. The woman stands back, watches, plays with a button on her shirt. You feel your body shutting down, bit by bit, like an office block's lights being switched off at night. You push the men off and tell them to leave.

Oh, come *on*, says the one you began it with.

He's different this time, you don't like his tone.

Just *get out*.

You cannot look them in the face; you stumble to the bathroom, the taste of metal in your mouth. You lock yourself in and sit on the toilet, shaking, and then suddenly retch into the toilet bowl, retch and retch, as if you are trying to heave your insides out.

The door outside clicks shut; they are gone. The room that's left behind looks cheap, tatty, forlorn. You go to the cupboard, need your clothes, warmth, need your lovely tweed skirt. Your bag isn't there. Fuck. *Fuck*. With your wallet in it. Your credit cards and driving license. Your name. Your address.

Oh God, not that.

It was the woman, it was in her face at the start.

Think.

You can't report it. You've already given the lobby your credit card imprint, good, good, but your keys, your keys: they're in your coat pocket, thank God. But your name, your address and then the quick hot tears come and come. You push to the bathroom, to the shower's strong hot water and scrub at your skin, scrub it into rawness and then you sag against the tiles and tears and water spill down. You slide to the floor and you stay hunched in the shower's palm for a very long time, weeping and weeping until you hiccup to a stop. You turn off the tap. You're still, and wet, and shivery. You can't think how you'll get home. A taxi's out of the question, you feel like you'll never be able to step into one again, alone or with Cole or anyone else.

They have your name and address. They have your name and address.

Your weeping, again. Years of not crying in it, it's all, finally, coming out.

Lesson 83

the importance of good food

You call your bank from the hotel room. You check out. Tell the crisp young man behind the desk you've left your bag at home, you don't know why you need to explain that, you have to stop, you're talking too much: he knows you're lying.

You have some loose change in your pocket; you ring Cole from a phone box down the street, you're sure he'll be working late. He is, of course. You tell him your handbag's been stolen and you're stuck. I'll be right over, he says. You go to a nearby Starbucks and wait, hunched over a hot chocolate, stilling your tear gulps until Cole strides into the café and you walk into his strong arms and the tears, once again, come and come. He holds you into stillness and then goes to the counter and comes back gentle with a tray of sandwiches you can't eat.

Let's get a cab home, he says, I've got some dosh.

No, no, I feel like the tube, it's quicker. I just want to get home.

OK. Whatever.

You walk down the street with Cole's arm firm round your shoulder. Why is he so good at times like this? Your heart is blown open by his kindness, like a window by a sudden gust.

I love you, you say, in thanks.

You used to say it every day, once.

Lesson 84

old linen is invaluable

Over the next few days you try and push the men to the back of your head, you must, for you'll be swamped by anxiety if you don't. You've got to get yourself in order; you've acted appallingly and it's time to stop the silliness, to tackle your regular life. You book a massage, facial, pedicure. Scrub the flat. Ring some old girlfriends, make dates for coffees and movies and lunch. Clear a space in the study for your laptop and books: you've never, yet, bothered to do that.

You throw out your pill packet.

When you are ready, when the idea of sex doesn't fill you with dread, you ask your husband to dip his tongue inside you and to curl it round your clitoris; it has taken you four years to ask him to do this, to ask him to do anything specific that you'd like.

I love those books, he says.

He parts your legs and puts his tongue between them and you turn to the windows and stretch your arms above your head and float on your back: Cole knows, now, that he must focus on your clit to pleasure you, he must wake it up. And on a drizzly winter Sunday you stay in bed for most of the day as if you've both never been married or never preferred sleep. His fingers run over your skin like a slow trickle of water and you curl and doze and kiss and nuzzle into the gathering dark and at the end of it you lie quietly and listen to his deep, regular breathing and fall into his sleeping.

Cole takes the Monday off work, he's never done that for you before. It reminds you of Edinburgh, when he wanted to be in bed, with you, more than anything else.

You're remembering him after so long, the man you loved. Remembering a time when the love was as clear and clean as a fall of Christmas snow. It was simple. You loved each other, you trusted each other, you weren't like other couples. Your husband was all-calming. There was no doubt like a sickness, no poison doing its work. You remember the innocence of it all once.

Before a hotel room in Marrakech, when your heart lurched.

Lesson 85

it is most pitiable that a woman whose
physical condition is sound be inca-
pacitated by a passionate temper

Another letter. You'd almost forgotten them. You can barely read them now, they reek of emotion, your heart and your sex have closed to him.

> You're soaked through my days. I cannot scrub you
> out.

You return to Cole, in the bedroom. Shut its door behind you, not sure why.

The phone rings, weekday mornings, his usual time. You never pick it up.

Hello, on the answering machine, hello?

Curled on the sofa, your hands between your legs, willing him to stop. Trying to forget it all, to immerse yourself in being, for Cole, the good wife.

The phone rings late, ten P.M. Cole tells you to ignore it. You know who it is; he's never dared to intrude like this in your life. You don't want your husband to hear his voice on the answering machine. You snatch up the phone. Pretend it's Martha, tell Gabriel you're tired and not to ring so late, you'll call back in the morning.

Your hands shake as you replace the receiver.

You tell him, the following morning, not ever to ring again after hours. You tell him that you cannot see him any more, he has learned enough. The lessons have stopped. No, wait, he says. You hang up. Your answering machine's left on and it's on for ever after that.

Please call, he says, the next morning, on the machine. We need to talk, to sort this out. I love you, he says, and it stops you as you listen. I love you, he says again.

How many times had you said *I love you* in your twenties to men who didn't answer? That's beautiful, one said, beautiful, as if he was collecting the phrase in a scrapbook, pinning it to a display board like so many butterflies. How many times has something died within you as the words slipped from your mouth? And now you're on the other side, doing it back.

But this is different, you tell yourself, it's for the best, you tell yourself. You're addled by the thought of the life you've been leading, in all its selfishness, but it's better, in the long run, this giving nothing back. You didn't ask for complication, burden, mess.

You feel suddenly ruthless and clear-headed. You feel a sliver of ice in your heart.

Lesson 86

those who take opium in the first in-
stance become so enslaved to it that
at first they can do nothing without it
and finally nothing with it

Gabriel is waiting on the doorstep as you
step out on a Monday morning, he's beside you as you walk
down the street. He tells you you have to leave Cole, he'll
make you; you're too cowardly to seize your own happiness,
you have to begin afresh.

Unpredictability is ragged within him now, he's unshaven,
he looks as if he hasn't slept: it confirms that you made the right
decision. So this is the flip side of the sunny actor who's always
on in real life, playing his part. You quicken your pace. Gabriel
catches up, he's almost snagging your heels. You tell him, without looking at him, not to come to your flat, not to ring. You
turn into the news agent but he's there right behind you, close

to your ear. You snap at him to stop it as you pick up a newspaper. You know the Indian woman behind the till, she always teases Cole and you about when you'll be starting a family, with a gentle, sideways dip of her head; it's become a running joke. But Gabriel is beside you now and you look at the confused smile on her face and you push past him: how dare he ram into your life like this. He steps in front of you, holds you hard by the shoulders, his fingers pitted into your flesh.

Listen to me, he says, listen.

Go away, you say, swerving from him.

You can never sleep with him again, can never see him again. Why doesn't he know that? You stride off. Walk round the block. Look behind you, he is gone.

Go back to your flat.

But what is this urge within you, this madness kicking out as strong as a horse in a box? You sit on the edge of the couch, your fingers worry the cushion's edge, you bite your lip. You do not understand this want to do it all again, right now, to run from the room's quiet and find more and more anonymous fucks. This urge within you that is brutal, terrible, masculine, beautiful, base, that cannot be stamped out, that is all, bewilderingly, back.

Lesson 87

the young wife's home! is there not in
these words a happy union of the tender-
est memories and highest aspirations?

Cole still wants sex his way, he's not obedi-
ent enough but at the moment you don't care, you just wanted
to be sated, filled up.

He forces you to touch yourself, he pushes your fingers between your legs and then brings your fingers to your mouth;
taste yourself, he insists, come on, as you press your lips together and move your head from side to side, trying to keep
him out. Mmm, you smell of you, he says, as he nuzzles your
face. He wants you to go further, further, not to turn back
from the path you are on and you ask him to slow down, to
be gentle, to stop, but he doesn't listen, he never listens
enough. Down he'll go again when you just wish he'd halt;
to savor, to recover but he won't stop, he'll kiss you hard on

the lips with his face smeared with your cum, it's all the things you don't want.

He's not like Gabriel, he doesn't listen, he's not polite. But you don't check his disobedience because it doesn't matter enough: so much of the sex is in your head, and he never has to know that. When he's in you, when his face is between your legs, you're thinking of someone else.

Who would do exactly what you wanted.

Who said you were turning into a different woman.

Who is not allowed back.

Lesson 88

how to get rid of bad smells without
and bad tempers within

Cole can't stay away, almost every night he whispers for you to wake and nudges your legs apart. You like sexy sex, he says, after an evening when he's bitten your flesh and bruised you in lovemaking as if he's trying to brand you, when he's flipped you over and fucked you belly down with your legs clamped together by his. Sexy sex, you murmur, with your arm resting in the dip of his stomach as he lies on his side, with your fingers strumming the hairs on his belly. His penis has returned to its milky, vulnerable softness, tender and spent and limp.

Sexy sex, and your fingers, suddenly, stop their strum.

Theo used to say that, you say.

A silence, for a moment, as taut as a wire.

I've never slept with her, he says, I've told you that.

She's the only one who uses that phrase.

That doesn't mean I've slept with her, Lovely, and Cole's suddenly laughing and tickling, it's all a joke, now that the sex is back, now that you've softened into being a couple again. She was always saying things like that, you know what she's like.

So you've seen her? Your voice is high and light.

Once or twice, yes. For a drink, now and then. And you know what, Lovely? We always end up talking about you, nothing else. She misses you a lot.

Well, I don't miss her. One bit.

She's trying for a baby.

Yours, you ask.

Let's just forget this, he says, *please*.

Sleep that night like cobwebs, in thin strands.

Lesson 89

disinfectants, and how to use them

A wild Saturday of rain, it's flung at the window like furious pebbles.

Cole pushes you on to the bed and flips you over and licks behind your knees and makes you squeal and kisses you and then turns you again and he enters you with a strange intent and as he moves within you there's a fluttering of tenderness; it builds, it becomes almost unbearable, it's more tender than he's ever moved in you before and God knows where it's come from but it's uncoiling something between you and you whisper in his ear, just breath, let's make a baby, for this, this will wipe everything out. To begin afresh, God, please, that.

Now?

I've thrown out the pill. We need to start.

How many years are there left, he jokes.

None. Come on.

To purge in one stroke, to distract. To punish Gabriel, to stun him out of your life. And to scare Theo off, perhaps. You gasp, delighted, at the soft spurt and after it Cole and you are laughing like newlyweds because you've both come to a decision, the most magnificent, surely, in all of life. You loop your legs above your head, tall into the air and your toes touch the wall behind you, spilling the sperm down. You make happiness come, Cole says when you drop your legs down.

Hmm, you say, your head somewhere else.

It's so weird, Cole chuckles over a cup of late-night tea, I found myself falling in love with you again just as we were breaking apart. You murmur hmm, and smile, and pick a thread of lint from his jumper. You're bemused: perhaps you'll now disappear again into the quiet life, refreshed and compliant, never needing another hit. But you wonder if those weekday afternoons in a city flat can ever slip docilely into reverie, if the whole experience can be obediently shut away in a box labeled Strictly Unrepeatable; with Gabriel, or anyone else.

You want a child; it's the only desire, at the moment, that's clear-cut. You are thirty-six. You need to start.

Lesson 90

Your palm rests on your belly. You feel nothing. You have no idea if it's worked.

Perhaps as a mother you'll be off limits to Gabriel, the good Catholic boy that he is, you'll be nullified, out of bounds. The phone calls have stopped but there's a prickling in the back of your neck sometimes now; you feel watched. You feel sure he's hovering, somewhere close. You never linger any more by the window. Sometimes when you're out you'll snap round, to catch someone out.

He obsessed about a woman once, he told you that. He loved her too much.

Would you really want someone who loves too much? How can you measure love, or indeed distinguish it, you wonder, distinguish it from infatuation, curiosity, crush? You'd always dreamed of being firmly at the center of a man's life, but now it doesn't feel right. It's like being locked in an airless, windowless room.

And there's a taxi driver out there with your name and address. Or a woman with a grubby shirt, who knows you in a way that no one else does, and how you hate that. What on earth made you think that just because you fantasize about a woman you'd want it in real life?

Cole is the one constant. Does every relationship define another, drag into the light the previous one? It's curious how your time with Gabriel has now reinforced your feelings for your husband, soldered you to his dependability and quiet.

Lesson 91

the desire for offspring, for whose
sake the mother is even prepared to
sacrifice a part of her very life, is the
noblest of our purely human passions

You make happiness come, Cole repeats, his belly at your back as you scrub the pans after a Sunday roast. You smile, say nothing. Out in the world there are babies everywhere, pushchairs, pregnant bellies, slings. A man at a party jokes that he travels home at lunchtime just to smell his newborn son's head, it's the most powerful, non-erotic human experience, he tells you, pancakes and vanilla and skin.

Uh-huh, you nod, and step back.

You read an article by Germaine Greer, that with motherhood women willingly endure a catastrophic decline in their quality of life. You read a scrap from Sylvia Plath's journal, that she would feel more of a prisoner as an older, tense, cynical career girl than as a richly creative wife and mother who's always growing intellectually. Did she believe this? Do you?

You have no idea what's ahead.

You want a child as an eradication of everything you've done over the past few months. You feel like you're willing a baby to have someone to love consumingly in your life, to fill it up. You've heard the horror stories, that it'll be difficult even to find time for the toilet with a baby around, to have a shower or answer the phone, that in labor you could be ripped from vagina to anus, that making love after birth is like throwing a sausage down the Channel Tunnel, that some men hate being with women who've been stretched.

All you know is that with a child your life will swing like an ocean liner changing its course. Which is for the best.

Lesson 92

the act of reproduction is the highest
and least selfish of our physical functions

*F*ive weeks after Cole and you have made
love on a Saturday morning more tenderly than you've ever
made love before, you vomit into the toilet beside him as he's
brushing his teeth, it comes heaving upon you in seconds. And
the next day in a café, reading but not, you're so nauseated
after a sip of water that you have to rush to the pavement and
throw up into the gutter. Something's drawing on your energy
in a way it's never been drawn upon before. Cole tells you to
buy a pregnancy kit but you want to wait until the weekend,
when he's home and you're both relaxed: you want some sanctity to the event. It can't be done at night, it needs the morning when the hormones are strongest, the packet tells you that.

You bombard the plastic stick with your urine, you piss hot

and strong. Two stripes. You shake the stick, they will not be shaken out.

So, confirmed.

It's worked, it's not meant to work so quickly. Women of your age are always taking months, or despairing years now, or forever.

There's a great spreading warmth as you cup your belly in the palm of your hand. Well, hello, my little one, tummy-tucked, firm in the world, hello. You walk out of the bathroom and Cole's nodding and smiling and enfolding you in his arms, so tight, it hurts, and tears are pricking the eyes of you both.

So, to be wiped, cleansed, to start afresh. You hope.

Lesson 93

<u>when unwell we required to be healed</u>

_____

_____

You call your mother with the baby news. She's not as joyful as you'd expected, there's a tone in her voice; it's a shock to you. You wonder what, if anything, you've done to irritate her. Perhaps she feels the baby will be limiting, that she's still waiting for you to have a bigger life. Perhaps she fears her own aging. Can't stand the thought of being called gran. Doesn't want a child all over again, messing up her comfortable world and forcing her to babysit. You sometimes got the feeling, as a teenager, that she was a little too eager to expel you from the nest: she encouraged you often to get your own place and, when you did, could barely contain her annoyance if you returned to wash clothes or use her sewing machine.

The relationship is always like this, up and down, best friends one day and not speaking the next. She asks how you're feeling. She says she vomited for the entire nine months. She says that having a child will settle you.

Oh, really?

You don't ask what she means by that, don't want to set her off. Generally you live in terror of each other, of the hurt you can both inflict. Something changed when Cole firmed in your life. Your mother knows where your jugular is and sometimes, viciously, goes for it, as if hurting you is a way of holding you. She used to do it, occasionally, when you were child. Like when your report card announced *lacking in initiative* and you'd had to ask, as an eight-year-old, what the strange word meant, and she'd reminded you throughout your childhood and teenage years and with your teaching career and your marriage choice.

Lacking in initiative. You hang up the phone and have to chuckle, wondering what she'd say now. You've been chuckling a lot lately; your mother can still hurt but not as much. For the baby inside you is flooding you with joy, is evening you out.

Lesson 94

*B*ut sometimes you feel a slipping, usually in
the morning, around the time Gabriel used to ring. A haunt-
ing, like a war veteran's missing limb. When you need it back,
the vividness of that time of the teaching.

Want, again, unfurls under your skin.

There was nothing resigned in those afternoons you both
swallowed in one gulp like an oyster slurp. There was a lesson near the end, the one before you walked out, when he
was holding your toes and saying he didn't want to lose you
for sex *was* you to him, you embodied it. The honesty of it
was dumping you like a wave on the hard sand and you'd
stumbled and laughed that it was impossible, how could a relationship ever work and anyway, all women had this in them,

not just you, all he had to do was find a way to unlock it in every woman he was with. To listen. To ask. To learn. There was a whole world out there and he was shutting down as you spoke and nodding, yes, of course and he was kissing you, softly, yes, tremulously, yes, as if, suddenly, he had no right to kiss you at all.

And now in the morning, around the time Gabriel would ring, you waver, you wonder if you'd been too harsh. During that penultimate lesson, as you said good-bye, you'd held his head in your hands and knew that you were already, then, beginning to let go; even though you couldn't bear the thought of it happening just yet.

Lesson 95

<u>the mother's moral unfitness is to be</u>
<u>greatly deplored</u>

A‌t seven weeks old the baby makes you vomit on the pavement outside the post office and then outside the news agency and there's no time even for the gutter; like a dog with its posts you mark your haunts. But it's joyous sickness, if there can be such a thing, for it's telling you that the baby's strong within you.

It's changing you already. You crave fresh meat and rice cakes and raw vegetables, fruit and milk. It drags you from your ruby wines and limpid cheeses, your peanut butter and pâtés. It spoils your taste for chocolate, the canny thing. It urges you to the freezer, to trays of ice cubes that you consume in frenzies of furious crunch.

And now we are three, Cole says softly, wondrously, one

night in the close dark. Yes, you reply, yes, thinking of the strange motivation for this child, its frantic, panicky kickstart into life. Thinking of Theo. You wonder if she fell pregnant as quickly as you; if she's been flooded with the happy hormones, too. It feels strange, in a way, to be embarking on this journey without her close.

Lesson 96

there should be free admission of light
and air

Someone hangs up the phone on the answering machine so all that's recorded is a click, and after being exasperated once too often you answer. Silence, on the other end, and the receiver is put down.

You don't want games, you have no time for them any more, you have something else in your life.

Then another letter arrives. It's hand delivered, there's no postmark. You're not even sure you want to open it; you hold the envelope by a corner like a detective with a forensic specimen, you toy with just throwing it out.

*It's me. I can't do this any more. I'm sorry. I wish we'd
had a chance to talk.*

That's it. You crumple it into the bin. Return to your
pregnancy book.

Lesson 97

filth fevers cause more deaths than either war or famine

You sprawl on the couch in the living room,
ripely alone.

Cole lies asleep in the bedroom.

He doesn't want to be intimate anymore, he's afraid of
harming the baby now you're showing, he's repulsed by the
thought of making love to a pregnant woman. That Demi
Moore, on the cover of *Vanity Fair*, it was disgusting, he's
said.

So, the lounge room, by yourself, and your fingers float
down between your legs, they circle and tease and dip inside
and tremors flutter in your stomach and then your fingers move
faster and deeper and the tremors sharpen, they shoot upward
into your belly and your chest and you can hardly breathe; you

grab at the rug and come like you've never come before, for the pregnancy is making you more sensitive than you've ever been, it's tuning you as finely as a concert grand.

You expected a life made stodgy by fat ankles and smocks and bloat. But as the child brews in its vat you're thrumming with life and with want, it's a halo of energy around you and you never anticipated that.

Cole stirs. Come to bed, he cries out, get some sleep.

Lesson 98

<u>patching is one of the most difficult tasks for unskilled fingers</u>

*E*xactly two years after the afternoon in Marrakech.

Theo's birthday, June the first, and it's marked forever now by the moment of discovery. You need distraction; you invite three old colleagues from City University to dinner. Cole's out with a mate from school, seeing the latest James Bond.

As you bumble about in the kitchen, chopping and pouring and stirring, the conversation moves through clothes, haircuts, colleagues, flats and then settles on what it always does with these friends: men. Megan tells you she still hasn't slept with her partner, Dom, it's been going on like this for eight years;

they've become like brother and sister. She's thirty-nine, she wants a baby. She's not sure what's wrong with Dom; he doesn't want sex anymore, he always pushes her away.

Could he be gay, perhaps?

No.

Leave him, you all say. Before you're forty-eight and still childless, and it's too late.

It's hard, you know, she answers back.

Then she turns to you, God knows why: have you ever been to a male prostitute?

No, you snort, laughing.

Have you ever thought about it?

No.

I really want to do it, but I haven't got a clue how.

You look across at Cath, conspicuously silent. She's your closest friend from work. She has one of the happiest marriages you know and two beautiful boys in their teens. She has affairs all the time, has been having them for years; and she has a lot of sex with her husband, Mike, who's blissfully unaware. It creates this hunger for him, she told you once, I just can't stop. I don't want to. Ever.

You always wondered what would happen if Mike found out. You wonder, now, about Cole: it's a reaction you couldn't predict. You shudder involuntarily as you stir the pasta, at the thought of him stumbling upon your secret life.

Lesson 99

You try your mother again. Want her close, crave her knowledge now you're pregnant for she's been through this too. But she's on a dig in southeast Russia, for the entire summer. She's working on a marine predator who terrorized the oceans one hundred and fifty million years ago and had teeth the size of machetes. Six have already been found and are still so sharp that several of the dig team have been cut. She's assessing the area around the animal's digestive tract for evidence of what it ate and has unearthed squid-like fossils and ancient fish scales, and is loving the work. And the hot. She tells you there's a heat-wave at the moment and the sky is a screeching blue.

It sounds heavenly, you respond.

It is, she says. Her tone this time is lighter, as if she's had time to give the impending event some thought. But then she slips in the fish-hooked comment that you might shed all your selfishness once you're a mother and you feel the familiar tightness in your throat and want to slam the phone down but don't; you need at least one thing smoothed out in your life.

You don't know what she perceives as your selfishness. The fact, perhaps, you've never expressed gratitude that she raised you for so long, by herself? You developed a defense for her barbs long ago: the phone is put down mid-conversation, or you let the comments pass, or you walk out. It seems so exhausting to stay there and fight.

What's wrong, Cole asks that night, something's eating you up.

I don't know, I just feel all at sea, I'm sorry.

Why don't you go and see your mum. Take a break. Sort it out with her.

You imagine flinging sun into your lungs; scouring away Gabriel and the taxi drivers with the hurting light, sleeping late, bonding with your mother, sorting out your life. The balm and quiet of a maternal retreat.

Yes, you say to Cole, yes, why not.

You call her back the next morning.

I'm not sure it's the place for someone who's pregnant, she says. It's pretty rough. It's dusty and hot, and most of the roads are dirt.

I just need to get out of London. Please.

OK, she laughs, OK. I can understand that.

Lesson 100

<u>airing is an essential process</u>

*T*o a plain that was once an inland sea. It's now crusted over with salt and the bones of old vessels leer up from its bed like the carcasses of the prehistoric beasts underneath. Fishermen had chased the water as it bled from their grasp, they'd tried reaching out to it with huge concrete wharfs stretching like fingers into the vastness. But steadily the water leaked away as the river that fed it was run dry by thousands of miles of irrigation systems, canals and dams, and one day there was no sea left. The skewed three-masted crosses of the long-gone fishermen now shout their accusation on the remains of the old shores. And the only people who still want to come to the dusty town on the plain's edge are palaeontologists, greedy for bones.

The single-engine plane skips raggedly over a dirt runway and then pulls up, ballerina crisp, at a terminal resembling a bus shelter. Its tin roof basks under a godless blue sweep of sky. An elderly man tends the flowers in pots by the door; he's keeping the incongruous colors alive with all the zeal of a pub owner in an English summer. He examines the single suitcase of the lone passenger who alights, the city clothes, the face. All you give him is a nod.

The smell of his hose on wet concrete plunges you back to childhood and you lift your chin to the sky. *This* is your kind of air, as dry as your grandmother's tissue paper skin and you can feel your body straightening within it. Your mother swerves into the car park in a four-wheel drive from the dig's sponsors. You haven't seen her for so long. It's a shock, the aging. The old man waves a one-toothed grin in farewell; all's right with the world now, you're placed.

As you're driven to your mother's tinny little prefab house you know you'll outstay your welcome. You wonder how long it'll last, if you'll have time to unwind.

Her clothes spill across the rooms, pushing anyone else out. There are suitcases half unpacked and piles of unsorted washing. She can't find a spare towel among the rolls of bubble wrap and bags of plaster of Paris and fine chisels and brushes, and she apologizes for not cleaning up. She's been alone too long.

But it doesn't matter. You want this to work.

The first night you cackle together as your gift of fresh Belgian chocolates explode like soft clouds in your mouths. Tonight's fine, for a couple of days it'll be fine and if you're lucky, a week. The plan is to sleep greedily by night and by day to relax and reclaim a simpler life. It begins well: the nuggety people in the few, spare shops beam at your belly. Well, isn't that something, say their smiles, as if this is what life is all about. You visit the dig site in your hiking boots and hat, and the team leader insists on you taking his fold-up seat. But soon you're walking the dusty streets churning and damaged and hot, rubbing at the old wrinkle between your eyebrows. Your mother's house seems to collect the warmth and contain it: the toothpaste's warm, and the deodorant when you roll it on. You'd always craved the heat but now, for the first time in your life, you buckle under it. The baby's changing you so much.

But not enough.

For even here Gabriel follows, even while you're swimming in the town's pool. You do laps every day, pushing away hard from the edge and stretching the limbs as far as you can and feeling the curve of the muscles as you try to swim him out. But every morning you snap awake to a day that's raw, with an unexplained panic churning in your gut. Your bones rise tired from your mother's spare bed as if they've been struggling with its softness all night, tensing against it, resisting it. And after six days your mother makes it known that she loves her alone too much. It's always the pattern, the sudden tightness in her voice and then the explosion from you both, and you turn into the woman who's rarely allowed out. This time, over a name for the child.

You could never use your father's, your mother says. You'd never want a reminder of someone as useless as that.

There's still so much bottled-up bitterness over him, after all these years, and you can only guess it's because they were once, consumingly, in love. Your father's often the reason for a fight, you're thoroughly sick of this cul-de-sac you both, always, end up in, it's been going on for twenty-five years. Your mother's jealous of your love for him, still, she feels your devotion was blinded and foolish, and she's spent a lifetime, as a consequence, trying to convince you of his flaws. He was always drunk, useless, pathetic, never did a thing with his life, didn't love you because he never gave me enough money for you, made it so hard for me, the words are always the same, ever since you were ten, and they've only succeeded in turning you from her.

Why do you always go on like this, you ask now, I'm so *tired* of it. Then, very quiet: If you don't watch out you'll have no one left in your life.

You're just like him, she attacks. Hopeless, hopeless, the lot of you. It's always daddy daddy daddy, and she impersonates the tone of your adoring childhood voice. You never say you love me, you never say thank you to me, you never think I was the best thing since sliced bread. You have no idea what it's like to live in the real world.

Your mother's words mean nothing to you now, they're the same phrases over and over again and they lost, years ago, the capacity for any sting. Of course you've said I love you to her in the past, but she never seems convinced.

She will not listen to you now, pleading with her to stop. You don't know why you thought that being pregnant would represent a huge, healing turning in every aspect of your life.

You fear you'll have this situation with your mother until one of you dies, this feeling that you're engaged in combat with her, you're not allies. You have to get away from the viciousness in her voice, the jab of her finger in the air, the fury in her face. You walk out the front door, past the spoil heaps from the dig, the crosses on the shoreline like the haphazard masts of ghost ships, the curious faces of the locals; you walk without knowing where you're walking.

You end up at the settlement's only public phone.

Change your flight.

Leave without saying good-bye. It's not the first time you've done this.

Lesson 101

You unclench your jaw as the plane takes off. Stare out at what looks like a desert of sand stretching as far as you can see but it's cloud, endless cloud. You have a black hole in your life, four days where you could disappear, anywhere, do whatever you want. Four secret days. If you were more reckless and courageous you'd call Gabriel, you'd curl up with him and not leave his flat.

You arrive back in London and go straight home, not knowing what to do with your freedom and not having the boldness to seize it. There's sand in crescent moons beneath your nails and in the folds of your clothes and your hair; it's scoured away nothing of course.

Lesson 102

the new mother enters, at the end of
the first three months, one of the
most delightful periods of her life

But over the coming days all the exhilaration
at the pregnancy crowds back, it will not be stopped. You're
enveloped by people's joy as you begin telling them the news,
it's lovely to share the wonder of a baby with a much wider
circle than just Cole and yourself. Old hands cluck and swamp
you with advice: see as many old friends as you can during
pregnancy for there'll be little time afterward, use disposable
nappies because life is too short, don't fight sleep, chant
silently in labor *my vagina is a slippery dip*, that it'll feel like
you're doing a very big shit, that there's absolutely nothing elegant about it and you laugh and laugh for it all seems so fresh
and strange and unique. And yet this is so many women's
story, since time began, the most universal of all.

There's no love like it, says a girlfriend with three children, it's like a drug; you'd die for your kids, you know.

You can't imagine volunteering your own life for someone else, having a love as big and selfless as that.

For the first time in your life you're gazing, naked, in front of a full-length mirror and not just registering your body's faults; for the first time in your life you're loving the way you look. Everything's growing and changing. The baby's darkening your nipples, it's making them silky, widening them. It's spreading your pubic hair and strangely graying it. It's softening and swelling your genitals, ripening them. It's splashing your skin with pigment, there are sun spots on your face and hands and a dark stripe running bold down your stomach.

Deep into the nights Cole and you joke about what music the baby will like and what its accent will be and its name. All you can settle on is Grain, then Bean, then Mango, following the growth charts in the books. You've heard of men who vomit in sympathy with their partners, who put on weight and get sick and are wrung out. There's none of that with Cole, although he sometimes pushes out his stomach with his hand on the small of his back and demands sympathy and loving and rest.

And is hit on the head with a cushion.

You're laughing a lot with him again, feel cocooned in your close little world. It's the baby, the shared dream, it's thrilling you both. You feel fortunate to have him so close. What could be more lonely than having a child by yourself in hospital?

Than loving someone too much?

Lesson 103

<u>virgin honey is the purest and sweet-</u>
<u>est of all</u>

A message on your answering machine after a routine doctor's check. A silence, you know it's him. Your name is all he says. Just as he was softening into memory, as you were getting your life back.

The phone rings again and you snatch it up.

Hey, he says.

Your breath catches in your throat.

How are you, he says.

I'm good. I'm great.

I'm just checking in, he says, wondering how you are and there's a laugh. What do you want from me, you ask, what do you want, and Gabriel tells you that you were becoming something else, you were like a Sleeping Beauty waking up, you were blooming, in your prime and it was fantastic to watch and there's a silence and then you tut, in annoyance, and he says OK, I'm going: take care, huh, and there's a click.

You pace the flat, rubbing your hands over your belly, gently rubbing and rubbing as if you're trying to rub something out.

Lesson 104

You vomit up to twelve times a day, espe-
cially when you're tired, and you wonder if it's right for this
to happen so often: for some women, yes, your GP says.

Cole holds back the hair from your face as you crouch over
the toilet bowl and swishes out the bucket by the bed and
wipes your mouth and puts his lips to your stomach, telling the
baby not to make mummy sick and after it your palms hold his
head for a very long time, and you kiss him, gently, on his
crown, in thanks, for you've never appreciated him so much.

You wonder what the baby will look like, if it'll be a
Chinese whisper of you both. If its two middle toes will be
fused, slingshotted, like your own. You wish for it your left-
handedness, your mother's smile, Cole's eyesight, his calm.

But still you vomit, as if you're trying to expel the guilt.

Lesson 105

young wives are among the most important
members of the community upon whose
health and intelligence depend the welfare
of the husband, children and servants

*T*he baby's turning you from your favorite radio station, you can't bear the dance beat thumps anymore,
it's pulling you to Bach. Slowing you, trying to still you, to
sail you into quietness. What's to become of you now you're
on the path to motherhood? Will you disappear, even more,
from the arena of action to become a spectator in life, will you
live by reflected happiness? It's the way of old people, isn't it,
and mothers. You'd always had a niggling disdain for them,
those disappearing women, weak, faded, blended in, you'd always thought they'd given up. Now, there's a disdain for what
you were: the career woman determined to cram her living in
first, who looked down on young mothers so much.

At night there's the three of you with your belly pressed into Cole's lower back and the baby between you and your breathing. Cole worries for the child when your belly fills with laughter, which is often, and when you carry bags of groceries up the stairs and pick up dirty washing from the floor.

Well, maybe you should be helping me a bit more, you tease, tossing his dirty underpants across at him.

And he does, to some extent. Takes more responsibility with the grocery shopping and the cooking, surprises you with dishes you never knew were in him.

I was single for a long time, too, you know: after an astonishing stir fry he's never done for you before.

You clap your hands with glee. *You* are doing all the cooking from now on, mate, you laugh.

Hang on, hang on, he chuckles, this only lasts until the baby comes.

Your love is knitting, like a broken bone.

But then the early hours, the lounge room, alone.

A city flat, spare and neat, like a monk's. Naked on your back, on Gabriel's rug. Your head rammed against the wall. Your fingers threaded through his hair as you push him further into you and you're beginning to move under him, your hips are opening out and you're thrusting, soft, it's coming up from somewhere deep within you, you're pushing his head deeper into you and deeper still until you're fucking his tongue and you want him to swallow you up, to never stop.

Pregnancy has altered the tone of your fantasies. It is not, now, a woman you barely recognize in your head, it is not some fantastical experience you'd never want dragged into real life: it is you, now, it is what you've done.

Lesson 106

the mother ought to secure the ser-
vices of a competent nurse and skillful
doctor as early as possible

The hospital where you go for the first pre-
natal visit lies in London's outskirts, it's grimly Victorian with
windows grubby and tall. In the corridors pigeons flutter
through bands of dirty light and there's blood on the toilet
floor. Cole's rattled that there'll just be a midwife at the birth
and no one else. This overstretched country, he rants, it's the
twenty-first century and it still feels like the days of Thomas
Hardy. He wants the best; you feel the umbrella of his ownership and protection opening over you and you feel a wave of
guilt, again, and you cannot respond, you just squeeze his arm
in gratitude.

But then at the first scan all the laughter returns for the
baby keeps on veering wildly from the screen, it's playing

tricks, tumbling and dancing and then there it is, with its little pod-hands and its strange fierce face staring, it seems, straight at you both.

Tears at this visual confirmation: no, you're not making it all up.

But when will you feel the little astronaut flutter in your belly? At eighteen weeks you feel impatient with its stillness, and it still pulls you into that deep, deep tired where you wake up weary and never find a firm footing with the day. You wonder if that will *ever* pass, if you'll ever feel normal again. Perhaps it's worth it never again to have the panicky loneliness of those Christmas seasons of singledom when your heart seemed crazed with cracks. A child, surely, is an insurance policy against that.

You ring your mother. You've chosen to apologize. You're so sick of the tension between you, the weight of it in your life; you want it sorted out. You must swallow your pride and say sorry. Even if you don't know what for.

She's so relieved you've called. There's such a sadness in her voice, it's as if she's been sad for the entire time you haven't talked and there's just a want, like you, to be friends. Neither of you mentions the leaving of the dig site, not wanting to pick at old wounds.

I just can't wait for this baby, you tell her. I want it to be my little mate. I feel like I'll never be lonely again in my life.

Ah, but you could be more lonely as a mother than you've ever been, she says. I'm not sure if I should tell you that, but there's nothing like heartache in the love that a mother can have for a child. A pause. Especially if that child rejects them. A pause. After all that's been done for them.

So, she can't resist slipping back, she will always slip back, she will never let up. And what of a parent rejecting a child, you want to say but don't. You tell your mother you love her, and repeat that you're sorry, and you'll call again soon. Trying to keep as much of your life under control as you can, like Sylvia Plath's beautiful handwriting that was so neat and contained no matter how wild her world got.

Lesson 107

<u>good drainage is one of the first ne-
cessities of a healthy house</u>

A t twenty weeks, you feel the quickening.

That's what your mother calls it and how you love the term: the child stretches and wheels within you and you can feel it for the first time, its lovely dance. Little seismic tremors shoot across your belly and you smooth your hands over your ripple baby yawling and scrabbling and butting.

Often, in the evenings, a sudden jolt knocks against your hand—the prodder!—and if he's close Cole will hurry across the room but the baby will have shifted and won't oblige a second time; it has a mind of its own already and then it'll scrabble with glee like a kitten with a ball of wool and *now*, you'll say to Cole, *quick*, and his hand will cup your skin and spread stillness through the child, it will quieten, as if it's listening to his touch. How he loves this child so fiercely already.

You kiss your husband, tenderly, on the softness of his lips. You feel sexy and womanly and want a man close but Cole can't be talked into making love; he fears ramming it, fears the child's resting too close to where he'd want to go. You can't convince him that it's not the case, that the baby's not the encumbrance you'd expected. So many people think of you now as just one thing: the carrier of a new life. You're not meant to be sexual, you're a mother.

Cole whispers into your sleep that you're going to make a lovely mummy and you smile in your dreaming.

Then jerk awake with a start.

Lesson 108

<u>it is wrong to relieve those who beg because it may be encouraging lying, laziness and deceit</u>

Saturday afternoon. You're sprawled on the couch, reading, newspapers and magazines strewn before you both. The phone. There's no time to snatch it up, you're too far away.

Your name, enquiringly, on the answering machine. Just your name, twice.

The voice saying everything.

Your eyes are shut as you think of that utterly disarming ability to love openly, to declare need in the nuance of a sound and what a rare kind of quality it is in a man; you think of how diminishing it is, that utterly honest kind of love that wilts you, that makes you vulnerable and soft. And makes the other person turn away. Then you think of Cole. Your eyes snap open.

At Gabriel crash-tackling his way into your married life.

Lesson 109

Cole simply looks at you.

It's nothing, you say in a rising tide of indignation, it's just some silly crush.

It's that guy from the library, the actor, isn't it? The one who's in love with you?

No, *no*. Why do you always think that? He's a friend, just like all the other library people, he's part of the gang. In fact, I haven't been speaking to him for a while because he *was* starting to get a little strange, all right?

And then you hear yourself asking and what about Theo, anyway, you've never explained that, you've never actually said what went on at those cozy little drinks. And why the *fuck* are they still going on? It's with a voice you've never heard yourself wield before with Cole, only with your mother: it's as if you want to rip at your husband's jugular, to have it all, finally, out. What about her, huh? Can we just get to the bottom of this—and there's an ugliness you can't stop, it betrays all the beauty of your rounded belly. All the frustration and hurt and rage since Marrakech is finally, finally tumbling out. You tell Cole that he's a fucking failure at his life, he's so boring, some stupid paint scraper, that's all, no world beyond his job and his flat and hardly any friends and you hate him, *hate* him, you don't know where all the words are coming from, you hear them slipping out and you can't make them stop and what about Theo, come on, what about her, you're stalking the lounge room like a hyena caged up and then Cole is behind you, he's lifting you up and squeezing you under the belly, so tight, it hurts, he's lifting you as if he's going to throw you across the floor and wipe you and the baby out.

Shut up shut up *shut up*, he yells.

You can see in that moment why husbands drive off cliffs and gas children in cars.

The baby, the baby, it's all you can say, pushing at his arms, trying to scrabble him off, the baby, the baby.

Cole places you down. He leans both arms against the wall as if he's trying to prop it up. His head hangs. You cannot see his face. You go and sit on the couch. You close your eyes.

A tense quiet hovers in the room.

You ask Cole if he's ever smelt a baby's head, you're not sure why you're asking him that or where to from here but you're filled suddenly with an enormous sadness, you're filled like a glass to the brim with it. He does not look at you, he tells you not to be ridiculous, why the fuck would he ever smell a baby's *head*.

I don't know, I don't know, you trail out.

You're a horrible person, he says.

You know it to be the truth.

Cole walks from the room. You don't move. Wishing, so much, you could suck all your talk back, wishing you could vacuum it into your mouth like a bubble of gum that's burst. But the words are sticking all over your face and your marriage, and you don't know if they can ever be scraped off.

Lesson 110

Cole walks out the front door. Slams it shut.
The noise hurts. He's never slammed the door before. An
hour later he's back, ignoring you in the living room, striding
straight to the bedroom and you do not look at him but you
wince at the short, sharp thumps of the banging drawers and
cupboard doors. Wince, but do not lift your eyes from the television. He doesn't speak. He's never played games like this,
he's never not talked.

The front door slams.

Silence in the flat. You walk to the bedroom. Assess what
he's taken. All his essentials: alarm clock, personal organizer,
grandfather's cufflinks, charger for his mobile phone.

Your thudding heart, your thudding heart.

You sit on the bed, in the heavy silence. You sit for a very long time and then somewhere within that long, long night you rush to the flat's window, to the towering out and look down at the far pavement and think of everything solid and safe that has gone from your life. You gulp the night air. Stare down the road. There are no people anywhere, no passing cars, no life, all is quiet.

You sit back on the bed. You can hear the silence hum, as the rest of the world is tucked up, snugly, to sleep.

It's almost unbearably lonely.

So, your life has come to this. This moment of sitting on the edge of the bed, pregnant, and utterly alone. It feels like your fault. What you did with Gabriel feels, for the first time, like betrayal. You've been excusing yourself for so long, for it wasn't you who took the sledgehammer to the marriage first.

But here, now, with Cole gone, it feels utterly cold, and foolish, and destructive. You feel a knot in your throat, the tears gather, you squeeze your lips tight.

You ring Cole's mobile phone: it's switched off.

Lesson 111

<u>every girl should make her bed and</u>
<u>tidy her room for her health's sake</u>

*T*he next day, no call. You ring Cole's studio to check on him, pretend it's business. He's out. You leave your mobile number. No one calls back.

The baby squirms and stretches inside you, seal happy, oblivious. You imagine having it by yourself, now, holding it afterward in the high hospital bed surrounded by clusters of happy chatty families at all the other beds, by their flowers and teddy bears and chat. And then there's you, smiling tightly, in the glittery alone.

He's never not called.

Lesson 112

*O*n the fourth day a letter arrives from Cole's
studio. He's in Rome, working on a commission he'd been
putting off. He'd mentioned it a couple of months back, a minor *Descent from the Cross* the Jesuits own. There's not much
money in it and it's not a great work. Cole had shown you
the photos and you remember being struck by the peculiar
twist of the torso as gentle hands lifted the body down. Something about it wasn't right, the artist got the physique wrong,
as if he was working from his head and not from life.

The letter tells you that Cole is, for the moment, un-
contactable and there's no indication of when he'll be back.
His assistant has sent it. There's no mark of your husband

upon it. You can't imagine him dictating it to someone else, something so cruel and impersonal and blunt. Your mouth is dry and your fingers feel light and detached as you hold it. He's never done anything like this.

You don't know anything now, what comes next.

You ring his parents and leave a message on their machine, asking him to call, hating having to turn to them for help. You roam the apartment and realize how lightly Cole touches it. You were always hounding him to clean up his mess: clear away his magazines, sort through his letters and bills. All that's left of him are little heaps of loose change and a pile of receipts and now, suddenly, it's not enough, it seems nagging and wilful to have reined him in so much. You wash his fugitive smell from the pillowcases and sheets, and instantly regret the impulse, once again, to scrub him out.

You want Cole back. Very much.

Your mother rings. I'm just checking up on you, she says, and at this unaccustomed tenderness the tears come and come, great gulps of them, your mouth is webbed by wet.

I'm coming to you, she says, just give me some time to organize a flight.

For two weeks your mother's at your side, ensuring there are always fresh flowers and making batches of home-made soup and filling the freezer with tubs of it just like her own. Making you cups of tea without waiting to be asked and exactly how you like them, milky, very weak; Cole has never, in all the years you've known him, perfected that.

For two weeks you curl up with her in her bed in the spare room; you haven't done this since you were ten. Your mother doesn't know the extent of what's gone wrong, just that Cole's stormed out and it's unknown when he'll be back. Her focus is getting you on your feet. You know, now, that she's at her best when you're vulnerable, spent, when things are falling apart. The relationship has been simplified to the fundamental need of a child for its mother, and with that, something vicious between you is gone, the fury is blown out. You don't know how long this ceasefire will last but you want to bask in its calm while you can.

She has to leave after a fortnight, it's all the time she could get off from the dig. She doesn't want to go but you tell her she must. You should try and work again, she says, as she waits for the minicab to pick her up. Get some focus back in your life.

You retract.

No, not teaching, she laughs. But you have to find something else to love in your life besides a child, and a man, because they'll always break your heart.

Ha! But what?

She can't tell you that. The minicab driver buzzes up.

I've started to write something, you tell her, I haven't got very far. It's a modern version of grandpa's old book. A warts and all look at a marriage—what a wife might think, but would never say.

Does Cole know, she asks.

No, not exactly. He knows I'm working on a book, but he has no idea what it's really about. I don't want to hurt him. I think . . . I think he'd be devastated. I don't know what he'd do.

Write it anonymously then, she says, as the minicab driver buzzes again. That way no one'll get hurt.

Lesson 113

<u>bank notes are paper money</u>

No word from Cole.

No phone calls from Gabriel, after the one that exploded your world.

But there's a new life force within you, competing with the men. Your stomach is public now, hands reach to it often and amid all the mess you're falling in love with a body not your own. It's beautiful and terrible what the baby is doing to you, there's a great violence to the beauty, it's fascinating, erotic, obscene.

How can skin stretch that far? Will it ever shrink back to what it was, or will it be rumpled and slack like a pouch?

You haven't taken your wedding ring off; you don't want the complication of that, it's too final, too abrupt, it closes off, in your head, the possibility of everything being sorted out. At least the money's still coming into your account but your mother's right, you have to find something to do that you love, to fill up your life.

Make the book work, if you can. It feels like your last shot, before motherhood closes over you and your own life recedes as another gathers force. And the money, perhaps, stops. For all that's happened to you, financial independence is the biggest thing you've given up. It feels too uncomfortable, now, being so beholden to someone else; it could sneak all the confidence from your life.

But Gabriel.

He whispers unceasingly through this newfound sense of purpose. You're seven months pregnant and you know it's wrong to want him, to plunge him back into your life. You want to call him. Time has wearied the intensity of those afternoons in his flat, but not enough. For the vividness of him is back, often now, like waves at a shore he's back and back.

Lesson 114

the worth of fresh air

A weekend away, in the Cotswolds, a girly indulgence in a spa hotel. Martha's driving, she's speeding down the narrow roads, she wants to arrive before the light completely drops. The sky's blood-red and gold in great bands of brightness; in London it's never like that. Or perhaps you don't remember to look.

How's the gang, you ask.

Oh fine, fine. Julian's just about to deliver, way before deadline, of course. Tim's had to give up for a while and go back to the building site; his advance has run out. Natalie, poor love, is on her seventh rewrite, she's at that horrible stage where she's convinced it'll never work.

What about Gabriel, you ask, trying to smooth the rise in your voice.

Haven't heard a peep, she says, but he'll be back. He's so good at disappearing and then suddenly popping up, you know that. I think he's in Spain, I'm not sure why.

You prop your bare feet on the dashboard, your knees cradling your belly, and think of the times in your life when you've been most free, invariably alone, when you've been vivid and alive and aware. Can you ever have that life again? Martha butts the steering wheel with her hand and says of course, just take the baby with you; women are always doing that.

Look at your mother, she says, traipsing around the world with her little bundle strapped to her front.

Yes, I suppose.

But you're not your mother. You feel an anchoring now. You can't explain it to her, a woman who's resolutely child-less, who declares that she can't get her own life in order let alone anyone else's. In a couple of months you'll never again control your life with the tightness you've been used to, you'll have to surrender to the will of someone else. A child will drag you into life, you'll have to participate as a parent.

The sky is shutting down, the color is almost gone. You tell Martha you haven't had the energy or the confidence to make proper inroads with your book and you fear you'll never, now, for you've left it too late.

You'll find a way, Martha laughs, if you want it enough. Write as if you're dying, I've heard that's a great way to mo-tivate yourself.

You look out the car window. The sunset peeps through the black like a rip in a curtain. Cole still hasn't called. You've rung his parents, told their answering machine it's urgent, three times. You've asked them to pass on that you love him. No one rang back. You didn't think they would. You're old enough now, and have been through enough, not to expect anything you wish for to happen. Unless you make it.

Lesson 115

<u>in rainy weather we may be able to
take only indoor exercise</u>

You're cow-slow, now, huge and waddling.
Your breasts have swelled from a D to a G cup and there's no
bra that's sexy or even black in that size. You're becoming less
you, more generic pregnant woman. It's sharp, suddenly, the
loss of esteem. Will you be diminished as a mother? Made invisible?

But amid all the uncertainty there's a knuckling of creativity. You go back to the library. Sit at your laptop, jot notes. The
baby doesn't like you working, it squirms and kicks when you
sit as if it's saying hey, swing your focus back to *me*. But you
can't, not just yet. You muse over the question of anonymity:
it has such a bad name, it's the way of kidnappers, murderers,

blackmailers and women who want to reveal something of their secret lives; lay themselves bare. Your decision not to put your name to the book gives you an exhilarating, audacious freedom: you could never write what you wanted to with your name attached, the personal consequences would be too great. You're so accomplished at suppressing the truth in your everyday life; of how you really feel, of what you really want. Your Elizabethan author, you're sure, felt a similar kind of constraint. Otherwise she would have put her name to her book.

He calls.

He's on the answering machine, you can't bear to pick it up, fearful of what he might say, needing to collect your thoughts.

He'll be home in a week.

No love in his voice, businesslike, abrupt.

The night sours around you.

So, no apology, no explanation, no hope that you, and his child, are all right.

You have one week, just that. One week to refresh yourself, so you can slip back into the wifely life, because isn't that what he expects? As do you. One week to spoil yourself, to act completely selfishly, willfully, indulgently: it's the last chance you'll have for a very long time. How many times in your past have lovers, who'd never returned your calls, suddenly phoned up out of the blue and pulled you back for a quick fuck. And you'd always, always said yes.

You want to live like those men, just once.

> *I have no sooner spoken of power and authority than methinks I hear some man begin to interrupt me, and goe about to stop my mouth with that punishment laid upon woman: Thy desire shall be subject to thy husband, and he shall rule over thee.*

Lesson 116

<u>how to treat ailments as they arise</u>

The next night, a Saturday. Desultory in front of a documentary about Edward and Mrs Simpson. A chocolate bar is unfinished beside you; it's brittle, not soft enough. Your mood, country-dark. You flick the television off.

The piracy of Cole's indifference.

You pick up your book; you're reading Martha Gellhorn— *I was only ever lonely when I was married*—and you snap it shut and head for the phone and your fingers trip over the numbers still too much in your head, and almost immediately he answers. As you hear his familiar hello again you feel as if your insides are being pulled to the floor.

It's me, you say.

Hey, he says, how are you, and the lightness in his voice

tells you all you need to know. His tone is unscarred. He's cured, he's moved on; your heart sinks.

I need to see you, you say, wanting to pull him down too.

He laughs. I'd love to, but I'm flying to Spain early tomorrow.

Oh.

The screenplay's really come together. I'm going to a fight on Monday night, for a last bit of research.

Good, good: barely knowing what you're saying, just wanting him with you, on the phone, not wanting him gone, not wanting this night alone.

So where is it, the fight?

Chiclana, this little place near Seville. It's where my father began.

Oh. Great.

Another time, perhaps?

Yes. Of course.

Your voice retreats.

So, he feels, now, that he doesn't have to try.

And you want him more than you ever have before.

Lesson 117

<u>how do people hasten death?</u>

An hour or so from Seville.

The last week of the pregnancy that you're allowed to fly.

You're not sure why you're here but it feels magnificent to be doing something so foolish and impetuous and reckless and rash, to stop all the censoring of yourself. You know it's wrong to trap him again but the thought's not enough to hold you back.

What valley of need is within you? To want to do this right now, with your husband almost returned and a baby, soon, in your life.

You know the answer, but you're not sure if you can fol-low it through: you're allowing yourself one blast of pure selfishness, before you surrender yourself to the needs of everyone else.

The bullring's ridiculously small, dusty, temporary, in the middle of a funfair's glary din. It's not like anything you expected. There's the boom and jangle of a sideshow alley on one side and a roller coaster hurtling its cargo of screaming faces on the other. Your thumbnail worries a line down your ticket. It's hot, the air's baked dry. It's seven thirty in the evening but the sun still has bite in it. The baby squirms; you hope it's all right. Within the ring there's an atmosphere with the grubbiness and sleaziness of a cockfight. Around you, on the rough wooden benches, are clusters of middle-aged men out with their mates for a night. You peer at them, looking for Gabriel in every unlikely shape. You're flushed, heavily pregnant, an obvious foreigner, you're not sure what comes next. You shouldn't be here.

Wanting him, just that. It's worth everything, to have such desire singing through your blood.

A tinpot band on the benches beside you strikes up a fanfare. You sit forward like a child, so curious about all this; Gabriel's told you so much. A bull trots into the arena, reluctantly. You'd always imagined the tournament beast as massive, black and glistening, hurtling its forehead at its enemy like a locomotive, but this one's small, brown, rangy, lost. You glance around the tiered seats.

In the ring, four young men dart about, goading and taunting and running for their lives behind four wooden screens. No one seems to be in control, not the men, not the bull, it's farcical, a pantomime, you weren't expecting that.

Your eyes settle on a shape that could only be him, that sharp angle of the shoulders. He's on the other side of the ring. Late, with a knot of men that look like family. Your heart pounds, the blood swishes in your head, you can feel its pump.

One last lesson, one last hit, that's all you want, before Cole comes back.

An older man enters the arena. He holds two long sticks festooned with colored paper ribbons, they're comically festive. He holds the sticks high in both hands and, on tiptoe, jabs them swiftly into the bull's shoulders, as if he's a conductor finishing an aria with a flourish. The animal's enraged. Its blood is thick, red, it glistens in the heat like spilled paint, it shines against his sweat. Gabriel roars with the rest of them. You're hot. You imagine him sweating, you want to run your tongue on him. There are little lightning flashes in your belly, it's like a sky playing host to a faraway storm. The atmosphere's no longer farcical. The baby tumbles a slow loop within you, as gentle as a whale. You place your hand on your belly, stilling it: Gabriel doesn't know about this yet. Foam plumes at the bull's mouth, it's tiring, you can hear its panting, see its blood, its bewilderment. The matador enters. He's small, ridiculously so. Dressed in austere gray, like a theatrical undertaker. His penis has been taped to his thigh, the trousers so tight so there's no loose clothing for a horn to snag, Gabriel told you that once and you'd fluttered, inside, as he spoke.

You want to stand and make your way to him, to break

into his tight little group, but there are too many knees to climb over. You keep looking across to him as he drinks the fight up. You've seen his intentness before: in his London flat, as you pushed up your shirtsleeve for his mouth, as you unbuckled his belt.

The matador lures the animal, forcing it to turn closer to him, to almost brush him. They're communing with each other, he speaks to the bull and you lean forward to catch it, God knows why, you won't understand. The band on the benches beside you strikes up an intermittent commentary like a lazy pianist at a silent film. The bull wheels, slower, and you can see starkly now its age. Gabriel told you the animals are never more than four years old but this one looks older, tireder than that; maybe they've cheated a little for this country event. The bull can sense defeat, it's worn out. The matador hides a small pointed sword behind his back and swirls, beautifully, and the animal stands and charges again and Gabriel roars with the rest. It seems so one-sided; you feel sick. You rub your belly and think of the life brewing inside you and imagine it panicky, defenseless, the odds stacked against it. You're not enjoying this. Gabriel had conveyed to you another world entirely when he spoke of the corridas: a world of discipline and daring and beauty, but what's here before you just seems desperately sad and you're stunned by that. It's cowardly. Tedious. There's so much stillness, watching, waiting, sizing up, panting.

The matador sights down the sword and plunges it into the bull's broad neck and then he arches his body, as bold as a calligrapher's brushstroke. The bull's enraged, it struggles, its big heart is bursting. It crumples to its knees. Flops to its side. Raises its head with the agony.

You've seen enough.

The animal's flank still heaves, its eyes roll, it has a look of utter astonishment: who are these barbarians? A dagger's plunged behind the crown, severing the spinal cord and finally, finally the straining head drops. The kill has been difficult, there's been such a big, fighting spirit to stop.

You look across to Gabriel. You stand, tall, you crane behind the nuggety men, you will not sit. He does not see you at first, he does not see you, he's talking and laughing and his arm is loose round another man's shoulder, an uncle or cousin perhaps, he does not see you. And then he does.

His talking stops.

He blushes, deeply.

A quiet, gentle nod of acknowledgment. Unbearable in its intimacy, as if you and he are the only people there. It tells you all you need to know: you won't have to work hard, he'll say yes.

He's holding the moment too long, the people he's with are looking at him and trying to see what he's focusing on.

Slowly, slowly, you sit.

Trembling. Wet.

Lesson 118

<u>never buy anything you cannot pay for</u>

_____

_____

*T*here are five more fights. You can't bear to watch even one more. You wanted something else entirely, the bullfight of your imagination: the thrilling sense of competition between man and beast, the beautiful cunning of the matador's dance, the bull's invincible strength.

Why do you feel so let down?

Were you expecting the secrets of men and their machismo, perhaps, the secrets of Gabriel, unlocked? The matadors have made it all too easy for themselves and you never anticipated that.

What is the shocking weakness in virtually every man you know well? The whimpering like children when they're ill. The need for women to ask directions for them. Help shop for their clothes. Book appointments for their hair to be cut because they don't care to speak for themselves. The inability to pick up the phone if they want a relationship to stop. Are the weaknesses you see again and again a symptom of men of this age, or have they always been there, and women, secretly, have always known?

It is not wine nor kings but woemen that are strongest.

You know one thing, as Gabriel gazes at you from the other side of the ring: he's not over it yet. A stopping and a blush told you that. But he doesn't know you're pregnant, he can't have seen it as you stood behind the men in the crowd.

Suddenly it seems so unthinking and reckless to act on the impulse to have him back; and just once. Men lure ex-lovers all the time—why, now, in the thick of it, are you suddenly so uncomfortable? You can't just walk away from your nature, it's following you here, yapping at your heels, calling you home.

You should leave right now.

He's looking across at you.

Lesson 119

<u>all people, very properly, like to be</u>
<u>considered respectable</u>

You make your way along the bench, indicate you'll be out the front. He's out almost as quick. Your heart brims at that: the eagerness.

He flushes, at your belly, he stops. You step forward and say nothing, take both his hands in yours, then move, hesitantly, to touch his cheek. He pulls away like a child from a mother's hand with its cleansing spit; he doesn't touch you back. He looks again at your belly.

Well, I wasn't expecting that.

It's not yours, it couldn't be, you laugh awkwardly.

I know, he says, too quick.

He takes your arm, he doesn't look at you, he's propelling you away from the arena as if he's shamed by all this and you're shaking inside, at his response, you're faltering suddenly, anxious, chastened. First-date nervous.

Gabriel, too, feels distracted, changed. Not as inky-haired as you remembered, worn. You see him now as a man who's stepped suddenly into that queasy time when he's not yet middle aged but no longer young. A time of uncertainty when mothers stop asking when their sons will find a nice girl and settle down, but begin asking others, what's wrong with him? And as you walk with him through the dusty, jostly fiesta streets you feel another presence between you. A new woman perhaps, or just his moving on, you don't know, but something has been snuffed.

He turns, he laughs, he suddenly kisses you, as if what the hell, after all your indifference, even with a baby large between you. As if just once, on this crazy night, he wants to remember what it was like. You kiss him back. Shocked, drinking deep, not able to read him any more.

You've been busy, he says, and you grin, shy, and look down, rubbing your belly.

Oh yes.

You mumble an apology for disappearing, mumble something about needing to sort some things out in your life and he says yeah, yeah that's what they all say, it's in his teasing voice and you're so relieved to have the old Gabriel back, you're tugging him along, come on, you mad bugger, let's get out of here, and he's laughing and tugging in return, saying wrong way, *mi amor*, down here, I've got a room, and you're both relaxing into that old familiar companionship, it's as smooth as ice cream slipping down your throat. Then there's silence as you walk the streets with the tender matiness of old lovers, not sure what's next.

So what did you think of the corrida, he asks.

It wasn't what I was expecting. I wanted all the sternness and beauty you'd told me about but it just seemed, I don't know, cowardly. Sad. I didn't like it at all.

Where does that cruelty spring from, from what deep seam within you? The cruelty that makes you say to your husband he's a failure in his life, to your mother that you may love her but do not like her, to your lover that a passion seems bullying and weak? Those who are closest to you are the only ones who ever see it, no one else would believe it exists.

You can *never* be satisfied, can you, says Gabriel, and his hands, mocking, are at your throat; a little too hard, just a touch.

Lesson 120

<u>modesty is holy and good</u>

W~hy~ are you here, he asks, as he turns the key to his hotel room.

I—

You stop, can't go on, the tips of your fingers press your mouth; you don't know why you flew to Seville anymore, why you didn't just walk from the bullring, from his life. This is wrong, this is wrong.

You're pregnant, he says. This is something I shouldn't be doing.

I know.

But I want to, he says, leaning close.

I don't think I should be here, you protest, you back off.

But you *are* here, he says.

He kisses you as soon as the door is shut, he crowds you into the wall. Take off your clothes, he says softly, breathing close to your ear—you've always loved it when he does that. You hesitate, look down at your belly, you remove your clothes slowly, your belly looms like a moon, marking you as taboo and there's a stirring, the baby, but you can't say no, can't resist the demand. Gabriel stands back with his hands clasped behind his back, he watches your body, he smiles at it. Then he drops to his knees and smoothes his palms over your breasts and your stomach, now drum tight, he nudges between your legs and suddenly pushes two fingers up, without warning, like a stick into rain-plumped moss. You weren't expecting that, the violence in it, it's nothing that you'd taught him. Something has changed, he's found confidence, he's surprising; your knees buckle. You hold out your hand for support, you're almost coming already, he's slipped from your grasp and you don't know why but it makes you want him to go on, and on, and on, to see where it ends, to not stop.

And there are three of you in this hotel room. Trying not to think of that.

You curl sideways on the bed, wait for him to take off his clothes. You, now, watch his body, it's always given you pleasure to savor it. The beautiful hips, the pale scar where his appendix was taken out, the small, silver crucifix round his neck, the pianist's wrists, the half-hearted hair on his chest, the long, curved cock. Gabriel drapes your body with his and kisses your neck, and you feel his hardness nudging between the crack of your ass and then you turn slowly, face to face and you see for the first time his concentration, you can see in his face that this type of experience is entirely new and strange; emotionally, and physically, it's an unknown quantity, a performance impossible to rehearse.

Item one: the suburban housewife.

Item two: the heavily pregnant woman.

Item three: God knows what's next.

You're beautiful like this, so beautiful, he's murmuring with his hands over your belly and your breasts and you should be hating it, you should be looking inward, nurturing, instead of raging with want but you're ready in that greedy moment to hand him your whole life. You can feel strongly through Gabriel's kissing and stroking that his lovemaking has firmed, he knows what he's doing now, the lessons have worked. His touch is competitive and creative, it's as if he's trying to wipe the memory of every other man you've ever been with, to stamp your skin with the permanence of his own stroke. You feel the heat of envy: what other woman has he touched, who's given him this confidence, this command? And yet the thought of other women thrilled you once. When you had him well and truly caught.

You turn again and Gabriel slips in from behind, you're thirty-four weeks pregnant, you shouldn't be doing this but before you have time to tighten against him you come, almost before he's begun, again and again you come, the orgasms are tripping over each other, they're seizing you up. You clutch his fingers and he clutches yours and your knuckles are bone-white and the aftershock lingers on and on.

I want to come inside you, he whispers.

It feels like a violation, it doesn't feel right. It isn't right. You don't tell him that.

Please, he says.

You don't even feel it.

Lesson 121

<u>our feet should be kept warm and dry</u>

At one A.M. or thereabouts he's on the ho-
tel couch and you're sitting in a chair in front of him with your
bare feet crossed on his chest and your soles can feel his heart,
its beat, and he bows his head and looks up, his eyes red-
rimmed, and that's when all the honesty begins.

I don't think I can go on with this, he says. I'm not sure if
we should see each other again. It's like a sickness in my gut, he
says, because it feels so good; but you're pregnant now and
that's sacred to me; I know, I know, he says, despite what I've
done. But I've got to get on with my life. You changed me completely, you were so vital to me and I'll never forget that. But it's
my life now. The work's all coming together, I've got a producer
on board, the script's starting to work, and then you're jumping

in and suturing all his talk; you just had to see him, that's all, one last time, and your voice is too quick and light, it's wanting to get it in first and as you speak you can read his heart racing through the soles of your feet. It's agony, agony, all this; he wasn't meant to be moving away at this point. Your voice is repeating itself, it's wobbling and trailing out: one last time, that's all, you're telling him, you'll be going back to your London life after this, you'll never see each other again, from this point on any connection between you will stop, it's over, it's over, this is it.

The great calm, the anesthetization of the shock when everything slows, even your heart. The shock at his rejection, and at you telling him there's no going back.

You're both silent. Your foot stays pressed on his heart. It's as if the two of you are waiting for something momentous to be said, but neither has the will, or the courage, to give it voice.

You're both still, so quiet. You hear the traffic outside, a siren's whine. And then, very softly, he chuckles: well then, I think I might try a Chinese girl next.

It's stunning; that moment. You smile at his words, it's an involuntary reflex, like when you hear that someone has died. So, a Chinese girl next, like a different chocolate from the chocolate box, perhaps? You shut your eyes: don't say that, please, you think, please don't be like any other man. Haven't I taught you better than that? His words completely change what you know of him.

You remove your foot from his chest. Because, in that moment, a whole other possibility has been opened up.

That he'd planned it all along.

How to shuffle off his virginity.

The goal: to find, in a café, the quiet suburban housewife. Someone who wasn't beautiful or arrogant or confident enough ever to make it difficult for his life, whom he'd never be afraid of, who, afterward, could be easily wiped away. Who would never tell anyone. And never laugh. But it all deepened and he hadn't expected that; his unassuming housewife was meant to be expendable, that was the plan from the start.

So he could move on to what he really wanted.

Gabriel starts to kiss you and you stop him, you push him from your neck, you tell him it's too intimate, you don't tell him it'll hurt too much. So, someone sitting alone in a café who wasn't too beautiful, because men are more comfortable with imperfection and weakness, it's less threatening, of course. He cannot see your eyes, the prick of tears that you know will not stop if you let them begin, you don't want to give him that.

As you step into the lift you hear him calling to you, wait, come back, I was only teasing you, but you don't turn, the lift shuts, he's thumping on the door, thumping for it to stop.

But you're gone.

Falling down the building, down, down, your head to the carpet on the wall, your eyes slammed shut with the anesthetization of shock; everything slows, even your heart.

Lesson 122

girls as a rule should refuse to lend
_____

_____

*T*he sadness, bone-bright, as you walk the scrappy, smelly, morning-after-fiesta streets.

He'll be a beautiful lover. You were a good teacher, you always have been. And you learned as much as you taught, and you'll always have that. If you dare to return to it.

You'll be jealous, ferociously, of any relationship he ever has. It'll be better if you never find out.

You'll never stop wanting him.

———————

In your hotel room you lie on your back on the narrow, dippy bed. You're not meant to lie like this so late in the pregnancy, it squeezes an artery, you've been warned by a midwife, but in the early hours of this morning you do not care, not this once, you need to indulge yourself. You stretch out your body and the baby wriggles and dances inside you, its hands and legs knead you like dough.

This trip wasn't meant to hurt so much.

You curl on your side. You feel God wrap his arms round you and tell you sail on, sail on, set forth.

You catch the first flight to London.

Lesson 123

the heart grows both stronger and
larger from the additional effort im-
posed upon it

*H*ome.

You open the door to a strange euphoria. You throw off
your clothes and scrub yourself clean and make the space entirely your own. Striding, finally, into the solitude. You feel as
if part of your body has been ripped from you, as if flesh has
been torn from flesh. But you feel powerful, too, for you're
free, after so long; the great burden of uncertainty, and guilt,
has gone.

But then the anger comes.

At all the times in the past you've said I love you and felt
stripped. All the times they never rang back. All the love affairs that evaporated, bleakly, into one-night stands. All the
times they've drowned you out. Drained your energy. Your

confidence. Stood you up. Walked out. Wanted a Chinese girl next.

The fury spits and sparks as you clean the kitchen cupboards and vacuum every nook. Martha pops in: it's the nesting instinct turned feral, she laughs, backing off.

Oh no, it's something else.

Lesson 124

<u>baby clothes have to be prepared and</u>
<u>various domestic arrangements must</u>
<u>be made</u>

You're busy at the computer because you
have to be now. The baby punches its fist up and you yelp at
your desk. It feels like it'll break through your skin, it's
stretched so thin. Before it felt so cozy-snug in there, as if
nothing could get to it. Now at your desk you look down and
there's a lump protruding to the left of your navel, a little
head; gently, you push it back.

Cole will be home in a day. The businesslike voice told
you that.

You have to work. You have to find something else in your
life. You're at your desk because you don't know what's beyond the baby's due date or when you'll ever be at your desk
again. You're disciplined, energized, not scattered and tired and

procrastinating like the old self. The words rush and tumble to get out. Work replaces pain, it pushes it out. You are calm and strong as you work, you feel lit. Being at your desk is an antidote, a balm, for it means having a voice, it means saying and doing exactly what you want.

There's much, too, to prepare for the birth. You've heard the word *layette* for the first time in your life and apparently you must have one. You're buying the big items now, the stroller, Moses basket, bath, and you wash baby clothes in powder you never knew existed. And all the time you put your hand under your belly, slinging your child into stillness.

You're astounded at the clearness and focus you're entering this latter stage of pregnancy with. And the passion of loss that accompanies it, it's sullen and erotic and wild, like nothing you've experienced before. The loss of Gabriel, of all that he represented.

You feel you've been hauled into another realm; you feel, finally, that you own your own life.

Your mother calls, asks how you are, she's been calling a lot now. She wants to know when Cole's coming back. You tell her in a day's time; you don't tell her you have no idea what to expect. You ask her if she wants to come and stay with you for a while, be around for the birth. No, she tells you. Oh, you respond, why? Because it's such a special time for Cole and you, she tells you: the arrival of a first child is a magic, miraculous episode in any relationship, and a mother-in-law shouldn't intrude on that.

You see, I know this, because I never had it. But I saw it around me a lot.

Oh ma. I'm so sorry.

Your heart cracks. For with motherhood almost upon you now, an understanding of something of your own mother's life is, at last, being unlocked.

Lesson 125

Cole's due back tonight. You have an urge to phone Theo, you're not sure why, tonight of all nights. You hang up at the second ring, want to talk but don't: her friendship was so demanding and with a baby you'll have to be more rigorous with your time. And there are too many months of silence to be explained, too many questions to be asked. You know if you let her in just a chink she'll be back in one great swamping rush. You won't be able to do coffee any more at the drop of a hat, won't be obeying when she commands *pick up, pick up* on your answering machine, won't have time for the late-night hour-long chats; it's all so exhausting, just the thought of her. And she's trying for a baby and you don't want to compete with her over motherhood: you can see that it's a whole new arena of competition among women. You wouldn't enjoy Theo comparing whose child sleeps the best, has more hair, smiles the most.

Don't want her, in fact, in your child's life in any way.

Music, your music, is turned up loud. You wrap yourself in your antique chinoiserie dressing gown that's too flamboyant and fragile to wear but tonight you don't care. You pour a glass of red wine. It's your first in so long and how smoothly it slips down.

The glittering alone.

A key in the door, just like the old days, when Cole would come in from work. The thud of bags set down in the hallway. He doesn't come inside. It's as if you both want to hear from the other first, to gauge the tone.

He stands very still in the doorway; your heart skips.

Did you sleep with him; it's all he asks.

No.

The lie comes out easily: you look him straight in the eyes, the good actress, the good wife, you've prepared for this. The relationship will not survive the brutality of absolute honesty, you know that.

He walks across to you, his head on one side. You silly old boot, he says, you silly, silly old boot.

The relief.

Your smile, like an umbrella whipped inside out.

You can't help yourself. And you cannot speak, because of the kindness in his voice, it's breaking your heart.

Lesson 126

dust must be removed and not simply
displaced

*T*hat night Cole holds you so tight, he presses you into the wall as if he's clinging on to a life buoy in a vast ocean of the unknown. His body's deeply familiar, there's a volume of experience behind the holding. You think of that love running as deep and as strong as an underground river. What's between Cole and you is so complex, changing, alive; the love ebbs and flows, it sprang from nothing, a barren place, and sometimes, at bleak moments, it seems to retreat to it.

But then it's back. Fuller. Faster.

You turn and face your husband, you kiss him softly, enquiringly, on the lips and he smiles and nods absently in his sleep. The baby's awake beneath your skin. You place Cole's wide palm on your belly and the rumpling stills, as if the child's listening to his skin, is remembering the touch.

That night the thump of Gabriel in the front of your head slips away, like a fish unhooked.

Cole stirs early, at first light. You're already awake, on your back.

What really happened with Theo, you ask into the morning cleanness. Perhaps, now, he'll speak, with this new cleanness between you. He does. It's simple and stupid, he says. I don't know why I didn't tell you sooner. He turns to you. She could see we were in trouble, so she rang me up and offered to tell me the secrets of keeping a wife.

I see, you smile, you raise your eyebrows. And they are?

He plays with the silver chain round your neck, he's always liked doing that. Oh, you know, he laughs, all that stuff about flowers once a week, and listening to what you want, and giving you lots of space.

Uh-huh.

And oral sex, he chuckles, she was very big on that. She said you were hopeless at speaking out. He pauses, he speaks more carefully. We became mates. We'd just have a drink now and then, after work. I like her. That's it.

He smiles, he looks you straight in the eyes. A rich silence. Your mouth is sapped dry. You hold your face in your hands, you laugh. So, your husband could never explain that he'd been taking lessons, from your best friend, on the art of holding a wife. And you've chosen to believe him. At last. Finally it's clear: first comes the choice, then belief follows, led docile like a hound on a leash.

So what does Theo really want, you ask. I never figured that out.

Well, she's desperate for a child, you know that. She's been trying for eighteen months. IVF, everything, nothing's worked.

Your heart reaches out to her; you must ring.

But you don't.

Lesson 127

cruelty punishes itself, as it should do
_____
_____

Two days later, a letter. On thick, creamy paper, so inviting to the hand. Your fingers run as deft as a lizard over the thud of the type.

> It's me again. For the last time. Please don't stop reading. Please just hear me out, and I promise then that I'll never write again. I'll never see you, if that is what you want. So, you are having a child. You are so very, very blessed. Cole as well as you. What a beautiful family you will make. My heart hurts whenever I think of the three of you, and your happiness. A child completes our lives, I think. It's taken me a long time to see that, that a life without children is a life adrift.

Your hand rubs your stomach and rests on a gentle protrusion, your baby's little rump, the midwife has told you that's what it is.

So, it was me who wrote the letters. It didn't seem so mad at the time. It was a way to reach you, the only way, and you were so hard to reach. It was a way to surprise you: in a good way I hoped. I imagined you reading them and thinking it could be any number of people: the guy you slept with when you were twenty-four and never saw again, but always wondered about, or the guy you never slept with, but always wanted. The one who'd be perfect for you, but you'd never done anything about. I wanted to enchant you in some way, I love doing things like that. You know that.

There's another reason why I wrote the letters and this is the really hard bit to tell you. Maybe I shouldn't be telling you at all, I always put my foot in it but I feel that you need to know. I wanted Cole to find them. I wanted him to doubt you, because he never doubts you. You are such a good person. He has told me more than once that he'll never leave you. You should know that. I've accepted it now. I'm in awe of his devotion to you, and the love you had.

As if a giant's fist is squeezing your heart, as if it is twisting it, as if it is squeezing all the blood out.

I just wanted you to know that I am sorry, for so many things. You've been such a good friend to me

and I don't know why I feel I have the license to be cruelest to those who are the kindest to me, and whom I love the most. I'm not a good person, in so many ways. Sometimes I do horribly selfish things. I can't help myself. Is there anyone who doesn't? You, perhaps, and look at what I've done to you. I can't imagine you ever understanding what has happened. I just had to tell you this, and these crazy letters seemed the only way to get through to you. Cole tells me you're still asking, you can't let it go. He'll never tell you. I don't think it's healthy that you don't know. I'm sorry, and I love you. That's all I wanted to say.
T.

You surface to great gulps of air, you break into the air and the light.

After being submerged for so long, at such crushing depths.

You lie on your bed, on your side, for a very long time, for the whole day, until the light softens and stops. What is the purpose in sending this now? Is Theo conceding? Does she want you to concede? Does she sense, finally, the battle lost? Is she bowing out with grace, or beginning a more insidious campaign?

> *. . . the love you had . . . Cole told me you're still asking . . .*

She's good, she's good, she's always won her fights.

The baby inside you shifts, as if it's protesting at the churn of your blood. You know all the tales of revenge; the prawn heads sewn into curtain hems and the cutting up of a husband's suits and the dialing of the recorded time in New Zealand and the phone left off the hook. Oh no, you'd want a more magnificent retribution than any of that, something that would haunt them for ever, that would stain them for the rest of their lives.

Then again, perhaps enduring will mean you've won the most.

She wants you to confront Cole, you sense that. To find out where he stands, to force it all into the light. You will not give her anything she wants. She's never suspected you were capable of surprise, her letter has told you that.

Lesson 128

<u>be proud that you are not in debt</u>

Cole comes home around ten and you are still curled on the bed. You do not acknowledge him as he comes into the bedroom, do not turn your head, cannot speak, your heart is filled up.

He takes off his work shirt and tosses it, playfully, across to you. It lands on your head.

Hey, he says.

You say nothing. You remove the shirt.

He will not know what you know about him; now is not the time.

Perhaps it will never be the time.

Lesson 129

<u>the motherly instinct is strong in us</u>

---

*T*he midwife tells you the baby's head is down and it's ready to come out. You read in *Vogue* that a boy makes a mother appear more masculine because of all the new hormones flooding into her body, and yet you read that a girl steals her mother's beauty. Can this be true? You cannot win. You're tired. The hospital's put you on an iron supplement to boost your energy and your stools are hard and as black as ink. You feel old, the baby's sapping you, there are vice-like cramps in your legs during the night, thrush in spurts of ferocious itchiness and too many farts. You complain a lot. Cole laughs and tells you to relax or the baby will come out as brittle as a tin toy.

I can't, you tell him, you have no idea.

He's so even, so assured in these final weeks and you would have thought once it meant he wasn't churning or smudged like yourself but uncomplicated, open, clean. Once.

Can you get any bigger?

The baby pushes and jabs with its fists and you can feel, sharply now, the wanting out. You're trying to get as much writing done as you can, with the little time left that's your own. Your fingers fly on the keyboard when Cole is out of the flat. The child still wriggles when you work, urging you on: sssh, you whisper, not long now. The overnight bag is packed. The baby's in position, head down, with its spine obediently to the left, readying itself for out. You can sense it, soon, and are nesting like a she-wolf retreating to the hills.

You sleep sixteen hours a day now, can't help it, can't fight your body's need. The apartment's spotless, all the new clothes are washed. There's a feeling of tremendous change coming, it's like the flint of a storm in the wind. You must rid yourself of clutter, live more sparely and honestly now, more in tune with what you want; you won't have time for anything else. And through it all burns something deeply physical, an urge that's old and wild and howling, something buried over many years, now out. You feel like an animal, purely that. You surrender to it.

Lesson 130

a separate life should be lead for three
months after childbirth

*I*t is the day the ultrasound has said the
baby's most likely to be born.

But it doesn't want to come, it's not ready. It's found a
comfortable position in there, resting its heel on your rib, and
won't budge. You can feel your body saying wait, rest, gather
more strength.

In the night there's a rippling across your tummy, below
the navel, like a roll of thunder across the desert that amounts
to nothing.

For a week, nothing.

Just occasional Braxton Hicks contractions, the wily, pretend ones. They're like a rolling pin over uneven dough, tight-
ening around you and falling away. Cole's impatient now, he

puts his lips to your belly and tries to coax the baby out. You try everything: champagne, nipple tweaking, pineapple, curry, raspberry leaf tea, everything but sex. Not ready for that.

Or swallowing his cum. You've heard that works. You couldn't think of anything worse and it's one of the things he loves the most. You never want to do it for him again.

Gabriel never expected you to, never asked.

Lesson 131

You awake at three A.M. with what feels like
a small gray cloud drifting across your abdomen. Like a giant—or God—is squeezing your belly.

You file your nails, for you've heard you'll dig them so
hard into Cole's flesh you'll draw blood. You have a shower,
wash your hair; God knows when it'll be washed again. Watch
CNN, ring your mother. And somewhere in there you're in
the bath that Cole's drawn and he's in the nursery ironing his
shirt because he doesn't know what else to do and he's never
heard you yell fuck, Jesus, *fuck* and in such a gamy way be-

fore and then you shout to ring the hospital, please, to get you out. Cole's packing the car and helping you into it and you're scrabbling at your clothes, trying to claw them off, you don't know why, it's some instinct all feral within you; to have nothing on your body, not even a watch, and at a stop light you're clutching at Cole's hand like it's never been held before, you're clutching bone. There are contractions like wild buffalo pummeling through you, oh God let the child come, come.

Five hours after the first clench in your belly, ten minutes after your waters have broken, the baby's out like a fish whooshing along a deck. You've given birth on all fours, with just gas and air to get you through it, and Cole and the midwife in the room. A textbook birth, says the midwife afterward. An easy labor, laughs your mother over the phone. You tell her that no labor's easy, that there was a moment during it when you felt like you were splitting apart, that there was a point where you said to yourself, very calmly, you were *never* doing this again.

You didn't know you'd defecate during labor.

Didn't know there'd be so much blood.

Didn't know that several hours after the birth your belly would resemble a child's attempt at baking a cake, all sunken and soft in the middle.

Didn't know such love.

Lesson 132

the moment any part of a living body
ceases to change, that moment it dies

Cole is in a chair beside the bed you've given birth in. He's sitting with his whole body curved around his squawly bundle of son, as if to shield him from the glare of the hospital lights and the midwife as your vagina is stitched up. Cole's face is cracked, red, raw, it's wet in great streaks with a teardrop clinging to the tip of his nose.

He is all wonder and love and shock at the little hand like an alien's that reaches up from the blanket and hooks on to his thumb and holds it tight. As if this is the supreme moment of his life, as if you hardly matter any more.

It's so odd and sullen, that thought. You lean and stroke your husband, once, in the clearing behind his ear, as if in apology. He smiles, he does not look up, he kisses his son's fingernail; it's the size of a nail head in his toolbox.

Lesson 133

Your son's skin is your new terrain, you ache for it when you're separated from him, you want to be breathing it like the desert sky during an English winter but the need is worse, much worse.

And it has released you, for the time being, from a spikier kind of want.

He's called Jack.

His face is unfolding. His ears are like two little squashed roses. His hair, smoothed, is a shell-spiral; ruffled, a corrugated lake. His tiny nails are soft and ragged until you peel them away, his hands balletic in sleep. His eyes are deep and blank and dark and seem to go on forever. Does he see you? You don't know. He sees your voice, you're sure of that, and your smell and your nipple, oh yes, that. You're exhausted. Transfixed. He fills every corner of your life.

When your mother visits the hospital she holds him uncomfortably, as if he's rare china; afraid of his fragility. How strange, you muse: she's done all this before. Maybe she's out of practice? Doesn't want Jack to cry?

When are you baby-sitting for us, gran, Cole teases.

Maybe in a year or two, she laughs, a touch too fierce.

Perhaps that's the key: she won't be comfortable with Jack until he's not a baby but a person, you'll have to wait for a year or so. Or maybe she wants you to stand on your own two feet with this, give you space. You won't push it. Watching her, you realize you have no right to expect her close involvement. As much as you'd like it.

Lesson 134

misfortunes are brought upon some by
the bad conduct of others

M artha visits you in hospital. Jack cries
when she holds him and you tell her to slip her little finger
into his mouth. He stops.

Wow, she says.

Princess Diana used to do it. I get all my motherhood
tips from the telly.

You both laugh.

Isn't your mother helping you, she asks.

No, not really. She doesn't seem to want to, I don't
know why.

Maybe she's afraid of being shown up.

How do you mean?

Well, she's always done everything so well in her life. She looked after a baby a hell of a long time ago and I guess everything's changed so much. Maybe she doesn't want you seeing that she doesn't quite know what to do any more.

You think of her holding Jack in her rusty, awkward way, willing him not to cry. Your poor, dear, impenetrable mother; she always hates admitting there's something she can't do. Perhaps, perhaps Martha's right.

She asks, as she's leaving, if you've heard the news about Gabriel. Your stomach churns; thank God Cole isn't around to hear the name. What contact has she had, you cannot bear to ask, you know you'll blush, you don't want to hear about a marriage, a wife.

He came back to the library, Martha says. He was completely changed. His hair was cut. He had this crisp new shirt. New shoes. He looked, I don't know, *proper*, respectable. And then Martha leans close, she speaks low, distinct: he told me he'd been in Spain. She slows. He told me he'd been getting over this absolutely shattering breakup. It sounded like it was the love of his life or something.

Your breath catches in your throat.

Can you believe it? I mean, talk about a dark horse. He didn't tell me much else. But, then, and this was the funny bit, he said that I had to help him find a girlfriend. He said that was his new goal.

You cannot speak.

I tell you, I wanted to jump right in there and say me, Gabriel, me, I'll leave Pat, anything you want, Martha laughs.

You murmur, hmm.

Lesson 135

<u>let us remember that in helping others
and seeking their happiness we are
finding our own</u>

You hear her before you see her, know instantly
the clack of those heels on linoleum. The determination in them,
the energy of someone who's never at rest. Then the familiar black
suit is striding down the hospital corridor. And the face, you know
it so well, every nuance, you know it better than Cole's or your
mother's. Of course you'll see her now, you've changed. You feel
powerful, more powerful than you've ever felt before. Like a real
person now, richer, deeper, full of juice.

Hello, stranger, you say, getting in first.

Hi. She's wary, one side of her mouth up, one side down.
You don't know why she's here, perhaps it's her curiosity but
whatever she throws at you you're ready, she can't touch you now,

it's in your smile. She carries a bottle of champagne and a romper suit that's too big, with too many clasps.

You both examine its complexity: I know about as much as you, you laugh.

God help you.

Her fingers are unpracticed with the baby, quickly she places him back. She sits on the edge of the bed and you hand her two coffee cups and the champagne cork pops. You sit without words for a while, gazing into each other's face. There is too much to say so nothing is said, you sit open-faced, reading the changes over both your lives. Nothing can describe the intricacy of the relationship you've shared, and not shared. And where, now, to start. Your son is beside you, asleep, you can feel his body warmth. His arms are wide, all surrender, all trust.

How's the breastfeeding going, she asks.

It's OK. It's working, for the moment.

Good for you. I had a client who could only do it for three weeks because every time the baby's mouth was on her nipple she'd have an orgasm. She said it was wonderful for the first day, but completely exhausting after that.

You laugh. It's good, in some ways, to have Theo back.

You're so lucky, she says.

I know, and then softer, I know. You catch in her face a sudden pain like a rogue cloud scudding across the sun but then it's gone; your hand reaches across to her. She slides hers away.

I couldn't bear to think about you for a while, after I found out you were pregnant. I didn't expect it to affect me so much.

It's just . . . and she stops, she looks down at Jack. I'd do anything to have one of these.

I can't imagine what you've gone through.

Yeah.

Oh Diz.

Nothing's worked. They've told me to give up. She's on the
verge of tears, she's holding them back. You lean forward and put
your arms round her; she breaks. Hey, you say over and over
again, hey. It wasn't meant to be like this when you finally met
up. You hold her until the shuddering stops. She wipes her eyes
with the back of her hand; mascara is smeared in black streaks.

I'm so sorry, she says to you.

You can't bring yourself to say anything. You just nod, you
won't cry, won't give her that.

We should get together some time, she says. When you're
back home. I want to—be a better friend for you.

Yes, let's.

Not sure when you'll see her again, not sure you want to
now, with your new life.

Cole tells me you still meet up for a drink now and then, you
say, nudging a response: wondering if this, too, was yet another
clever lie.

I won't sleep with him, all right, she snaps, heat flaming her
cheeks and she looks down again at Jack. It tells you nothing.
You tilt your face to the ceiling, you smile: it doesn't matter any
more, she can't touch you, can't wound you. You're living, now,
a much larger life. And in that moment of holding your face to
the ceiling with your eyes shut, all the tension of uncertainty
that's been with you since Theo's letter—about what you'll do,

about how you'll proceed from this point—is at last snapped and decision is falling over you like soft rain. And Theo knows nothing of that. You drop your head, you smile serenely at her.

Your son lies beside you; the warm, firm wedge of him, and she will never have that. Finally, finally, there's something you have that she will not.

Lesson 136

*the mother has now received the very
crown of womanhood, and in the con-
templation and care of her child she
feels that she herself is new born into
a world of delight*

You write in twenty-minute bursts, once a
day, twice if you're lucky. It's all that Jack will allow you. You
sit at your desk in that wonderfully clear, bright, curious time
in the morning when his day hasn't been corrupted by nappy
changes and wind and too little sleep.

Six weeks after the birth, flowers still fill the flat, blous-
ing out and tumbling petals. The rooms have the gentle, new
glow of the just married. You're still bleeding, just. Your genitals still smell meaty and fleshy. Your stomach muscle's split,
a line of pigment still dissects it. Your breasts have ballooned
and dropped and are marbled with blue veins like river lines

on a map and when you go to the toilet it feels ragged and loose, and it's agony if urine splashes the wound, your whole body winces at the shock. You're constipated, badly. The muscle's ripped at the back of your vagina and you've been told it'll heal with a hard line of scar tissue and you may be incontinent in later life. None of this matters.

Such love.

The rapture, the rapture of that.

He's soaked into your fingers, nails, clothes, sheets, hair. You've never known another body so intimately. The smell of his milky breath, the palms of his hands, the powdery folds of his groin. You're jealous of his sleep, for it takes him from you. Cole offers to feed him sometimes, to give you a break, and Jack suckles the bottle of your expressed milk as furiously as a calf with a teat. You sleep by your son as close as a lover, your arm round him, face to face, and your nipples drip watery, blue-white milk. Sometimes you think that he's a succubus, that all you are is a feeding machine and you retract from his voracity. But then he smiles and the love you feel is again wild, out of control, it's bigger than you. Germaine, poor love, was wrong: this isn't a catastrophic decline in your quality of life, it's living made luminous.

You've found a kind of peace with him, especially when you're feeding. You've shed all that's extraneous because, simply, there's no time any more. You lose yourself staring in whole gold days of him. You know, now, why a man travels home in his lunchtime for his child. Jack's head smells so strongly of the briny shoreline, of rockpools during low tide and as you sit there holding him, breathing him in, you are back, suddenly, to summer holidays long ago, to the sky and the ocean and salt and sand. The most powerful non-erotic smell, oh yes. You feel drugged within this wondrous little world, this babymoon in which nothing, for the moment, is allowed to intrude.

Lesson 137

every day brings fresh delight in conscious strengthening of body and de-
velopment of mind

A cheap pizzeria round the corner from your flat. Cole sits before you and Jack is asleep in his car seat at your side, propped on a seat. Cole straightens his little hat. You appreciate your husband for different reasons now; for changing a nappy without complaint, drying his son so carefully after a bath, holding him into quiet.

Goodness knows when you'll make love with Cole again, the want has shriveled from your life as suddenly as it exploded forth and you don't know when, if ever, it'll be back. You feel no sadness, it's just a fact. At this point you cannot tolerate lust and nurturing at the same time. Your fantasies have completely gone. You miss them, but suddenly you can't conjure them out of thin air. You're sure, one day, they'll return; you hope.

Jack wakes and stretches his body as completely as a puppy, his arms over his head and his fists balled. You're overwhelmed by the crush of love surrounding him. It's ferocious, the rush of joy, the tenderness of family and friends and strangers surrounding the newborn. God bless the little one says a waiter at the restaurant as you leave and it fills your heart. You smile out loud as you walk down the street, it bursts from you, you cannot hold it in.

Lesson 138, the last

*G*abriel, in the street.

You're wheeling the stroller beside Cole, you've been shopping at Baby Gap. The two of you are squabbling, Cole wants you to put on Jack's coat but you know he's warm enough.

Then this.

You catch each other's eyes, you pass each other without a flicker of recognition, just as you'd promised each other once.

But you both turn back. He smiles secrets at you, for a fleeting moment.

The crowd closes over you, and he's gone.

———

Your thudding heart, your thudding heart.

Cole bends at the stop light and buttons on Jack's coat. You smile, you say nothing. Thinking of the book you've been writing; you've done all that is in it but your husband will never know, for you are the good wife. This is how you will choose to end it: you are standing on a street corner, a picture of domesticity in your pink skirt and cloche hat with a stroller before you and husband by your side and in that moment you feel as strong and resilient as mercury but no one would ever guess. Your outside and insides do not match, and how you love that. A great gleeful happiness comes over your day. You think of your anonymous Elizabethan friend who's been with you for so long, pushing you on. You're telling her the story of a strange, glittery time in your life. There's no other time worth talking about yet.

Postscript

And there the manuscript ends. To this date my daughter's whereabouts are unknown. My grandson's stroller was also found by the cliff, but no bodies were ever recovered.

Insights,
Interviews
& More . . .

Meet the Author

The author of the daringly revealing novel *The Bride Stripped Bare* reveals her loves and fears.

....

What is your idea of perfect happiness?

Being immersed within my family, somewhere wild by the sea, having just completed a novel I'm satisfied with.

....

What is your greatest fear?

That my children will be hurt.

....

Which living person do you most admire?

My husband, for putting up with me.

....

What objects do you always carry with you?

A notebook, an old Waterman pen and a lipstick.

....

What single thing would improve the quality of your life?

More sleep.

....

What is the most important lesson life has taught you?

Don't let people fool you into giving up; have the courage to follow your heart and do what you really want to do.

Nikki Gemmell

FRANCESCO GUIDICINI

Which writer has had the greatest influence on your work?

Michael Ondaatje.

Do you have a favorite children's book?

To Kill a Mockingbird by Harper Lee.

Where is your favorite café/ restaurant?

Anywhere that lets me write. At the moment it's Starbucks, because I can work for several hours on just a Chai tea and a muffin. I'm sure they loathe customers like me.

Where do you go for inspiration?

Anywhere that's quiet, where I can be alone.

Do you have any pet hates?

People who are heart sinkers (as opposed to heart lifters): small, ugly-spirited people who want to drag others down.

Which book do you wish you had written?

Jane Eyre.

What are you writing at the moment?

A sequel to *The Bride Stripped Bare*.

Nikki Gemmell's Top Ten Favorite Books

1. **The Lover**
   Marguerite Duras

2. **Beloved**
   Toni Morrison

3. **Poems**
   Robert Browning

4. **Wuthering Heights**
   Emily Brontë

5. **Atomised**
   Michel Houellebecq

6. **The Great Gatsby**
   F. Scott Fitzgerald

7. **Collected Poems**
   Les Murray

8. **By Grand Central Station I Sat Down and Wept**
   Elizabeth Smart

9. **Coming Through Slaughter**
   Michael Ondaatje

10. **The Man Who Loved Children**
    Christina Stead

Behind the Scenes

Is this novel "literary pornography"?

NIKKI GEMMELL: Goodness no. It's basically a very honest take on sex, from a woman's perspective. When I think of porn I think of something mechanical, bleak, unreal, ugly, and with an utter absence of tenderness. Porn strips sex of mystery, of reverence and transcendence. It's sex with no light in it and I wanted to write about sex that's bursting with light and life. So *Bride*, in a way, is the opposite of pornography. I hoped to write a book that was startlingly real—with all the messiness and magic of life as we know it.

The Bride Stripped Bare was originally published anonymously, and you were put under siege by the media when you were outed as the novel's author. You were also criticized by some who thought that, for all its talk of woman's sexual liberation, this is a very conventional novel, one reviewer suggesting that your protagonist should have liberated herself by getting a divorce lawyer. Does any of this criticism bother you?

NIKKI GEMMELL: I can't really comment as I didn't read any of the hoo-ha surrounding the book. This was because I wrote it in a bubble of isolation, and dreamed of just walking away from it when it was published and resuming my life (a little like a mother who's adopted out a child). When the book came out I tried to stick to the original intention as much as possible, so I have no idea what commentators have said. Perhaps some people just didn't get it. The whole point of the book is the protagonist's very conventionality—I wanted her to be any woman and every woman, with a very commonplace story. I hoped that was where the power of the book lay.

All I seem to get are readers' reactions to the unflinching honesty of the book. It's an aspect of it that many readers have responded to passionately, and it makes my heart lift. They get it. I'm glad I wrote *Bride* now, although I certainly wasn't when my name was first attached to it. But so many women have said to me things like "thank you for writing our words" that it's made me realize these things needed to be said, by someone.

....

The title of the novel and its unnamed protagonist, as well as your intention to publish it anonymously, suggest that, for you, anonymity in sexual matters allows for more authenticity. Do you think that anonymity is a sign of liberation or a symptom of repression?

NIKKI GEMMELL: Anonymity is a sign of liberation. It's hard, in a relationship, to be completely honest, to show your partner your secret self. Vita Sackville-West described herself as an iceberg and said her husband could only see what was above the water's surface—he had no idea of the huge mass below. She speculated it was the reason their marriage worked. What relationship could survive the shock of absolute candor?

....

But is Sackville-West right, then? Is the cargo of secrets underneath that iceberg indispensable in relationships, as it is for your bride?

NIKKI GEMMELL: Gabriel García Márquez said that everyone has three lives: a public one, a private one and a secret one. The latter is rarely revealed. With *Bride* I wanted to strip bare the secret life of an everyday woman, and be utterly ruthless about that. I wanted to reveal the complex underbelly of her sexuality, in all its beauty and ugliness. I think the jolt of the book lies in the woman's very ordinariness. She's not a Catherine Millet by any means. She's the woman you don't give a second glance to as she walks down an aisle in the supermarket; the woman who has completely disappeared into being "the little wife."

For years I'd found it difficult to be completely sexually honest. Why is it still so hard for some women, basking in the glow of so many feminist advances, to be more candid about sex? To say such simple things to our sexual partners as, "No, I didn't have an orgasm," or "Sometimes I find it monotonous when you make love to me," or "Sometimes it hurts." Why ▶

Behind the Scenes *(continued)*

◀ are so many women still so subservient to their partner's pleasure at the expense of their own? Because we don't want men to turn away from us, perhaps. Because we want our partners to think we're someone else. Because sometimes we're willing to put up with a lot: to snare a relationship, to keep it steady, to have children.

I loved the idea of writing a book that dived under the surface of a woman's life, a seemingly contentedly married woman, and explored her secret world—with ruthless honesty. In *The Bride Stripped Bare*, I wanted to say all those things we may think but never say: especially to our lovers. I'd fully intended putting my name to the book when I began it. But six months into the project the text just wasn't singing—I was censoring myself. Afraid of too much honesty, of showing too much vulnerability. And afraid of hurting people close to me. I'm a wife and a mother of two young boys, not to mention the daughter of two gently bewildered people in their sixties. I didn't want people judging them.

But I was judging the dishonesty in my own life most of all. The aim was to be as merciless in print as a Chuck Close painting or a Ron Mueck sculpture—but as far as I know, those artists do not often turn their extremely critical eye upon themselves. Now I know why. I'm not someone who's completely relaxed about nudity; I've never been comfortable in a bikini. And like many women in a swimsuit I'm afraid of revealing too much. But when the idea of anonymity came to me, everything clicked. I was suddenly like a woman on a foreign beach who's confident she doesn't know a soul and parades her body loudly and joyously without worrying what anyone thinks of her. I'd opened a door to a reckless, exhilarating new world and could say whatever I wanted. I could be ridiculously honest. It felt wonderful, powerful—an enormous relief.

I'm far from unique in finding anonymity liberating when it comes to sex. A survey last year in the *Journal of Sex Research* found women lied more often than men about sex—and their answers changed dramatically when they believed they were answering anonymously. Embellishments under their own names included reducing the number of partners they'd had and lying about the use of pornography. The respondents were extremely sensitive to social expectations about how they were meant to behave. Anonymity was liberating for them, as it was for me.

When I sat at my writing desk I entered this strange, liberating psychological state of secrecy; it was as if I was stepping out of my everyday self and becoming someone much more confident and in control. Anonymity also meant I wasn't afraid of *The Bride Stripped Bare* failing. It seemed such a strange hybrid of novel, memoir, treatise and sex manual, and I wasn't sure it worked. I was a very new mother at the time and had lost my professional confidence. My brain didn't work in the way it used to. My previous novel, *Love Song*, had gone to sixty drafts over several intensive years and I just didn't have the stamina to work that way again.

Anonymity was also my way of trying to divorce myself from feeling over this book. I've always cared too much about my novels and now I have babies to care about. At the moment there's no room in my heart for both. The plan was to adopt out this new baby in my life, to absolve myself from caring. I didn't want the burden of worrying about it too much.

I wrote *Bride* in a kind of trance of exhilaration and glee—it felt incredibly empowering to finally tell the truth. Virginia Woolf described anonymity as a "refuge" for women writers. "Publicity in women is detestable," she wrote. "Anonymity runs in their blood. The desire to be veiled still possesses them." I could only write this book by being veiled. It is still difficult to talk about it publicly, eighteen months after being unmasked.

Bride is also a response to another anonymous text, a mysterious seventeenth-century document known as *Woeman's Worth*. Its tone is boldly sexual, its honesty shocking, and its authorship disputed. Germaine Greer believes it was written by a man close to his mother; others say it was by an anonymous housewife. I choose to believe the latter, and loved the idea of a twenty-first-century housewife also writing a secret book under the nose of her husband. Saying all those things she may think but never say—even in this sexually liberated day and age. And I've discovered, through writing *The Bride Stripped Bare*, that honesty is the most shocking thing of all.

....

It's unusual that your novel is woven together with a four-hundred-year-old book. What were you aiming for by having the bride self-consciously decide that she must respond to it? I mean, there's more here than just a curious historical angle in an otherwise modern narrative, isn't there?

NIKKI GEMMELL: I'm fascinated by this book [*Woeman's Worth*]. I first read about it in *The Times*, in an article speculating on the nature of its anonymity. I thought, "Ah-hah, that's delicious; now I've got my key! I'll write a response to this text. My book, too, will be written by an anonymous housewife." I loved the boldly subversive, almost cheeky tone of the seventeenth-century text—and I recognized it. The author could ▶

Behind the Scenes (*continued*)

◀ only have written these charged, highly subversive sexual declarations in secret. I wanted to say to the author, Hey, it's four hundred years later and women have come a long way—but actually, not so far in some matters. I was intrigued that this seventeenth-century writer seemed to have more confidence, sexually, than a woman in the twenty-first century who's lived through several decades of feminist advances, not to mention *Sex and the City*.

....

At one point the protagonist refers to "the churn of a secret life" and the "desire to crash catastrophe into your world." Where does this desire come from? Do you see it as more of an imaginative, and therefore fleeting, inclination or is it a real need that must be acted upon?

NIKKI GEMMELL: My bride is the quintessential "good wife"—a woman who's lived a marriage of capitulation, who's now in her mid-thirties and stepping to the side of her own life. It's as if all the spark and vividness and loudness of her youth is being rubbed out. She's aware of this but feels powerless to alter the situation. It doesn't stop her, though, from desiring a way of "crashing catastrophe" into her life in some way. My protagonist eventually finds a way of breaking out, of feeling fully alive and empowered and in control. A lot of women don't.

Another reason for the anonymity was that I wanted *The Bride Stripped Bare* to be about every woman and any woman in a sense. I hated the idea of my own name—any individual's name—being attached to it. For it becomes much easier then to dismiss the book as "just so-and-so's thoughts." I dreamed of something much more subversive than that. I loved the idea of a husband, any husband, flipping through *Bride* in a bookstore and thinking, "Oh my God, did my wife write this? Is this what she really thinks?"

....

At one point in the novel, the narrator is in bed alone one night and she starts thinking, and what she thinks of—"A group of men watching you being penetrated by a broom handle. You don't know any of the perpetrators very well. It's never intimate or tender. It's filmed. Sometimes women will be watching the penetration; by candlesticks, by animals, sometimes the women will be participating. And the men. Hands will be running over your naked body, parting your legs, probing, slipping inside"—this is a rhetorical land mine. For your otherwise gentle narrator and for those of us living in real time, what does having thoughts that are "never intimate or tender" offer?

NIKKI GEMMELL: I wanted this to be unflinchingly honest about some of the murkier aspects of womanhood—the raw, visceral reality under the seemingly demure exterior. It's a deeply secret world. Women do not talk about it with other women, let alone to male partners. "The whole business of eroticism is to strike at the inmost core of the living being . . . to destroy the self-contained character of the participators as they are in their normal lives," Georges Bataille wrote. We're all at our most vulnerable when it comes to sex; it's the closest we get to revealing our true selves in all our banality, ugliness, brutality and foolishness. The intrigue lies in the glimpses behind the masks we all wear in our public lives.

I'm fascinated by the tension between contradictory erotic forces within women, an ambivalence that's long cast its spell. Freud cherished it in the Mona Lisa: "[A] contrast between reserve and seduction, and between the most devoted tenderness and a sensuality that is ruthlessly demanding." I wanted to strip bare an utterly ordinary woman's secret, dirty world, to reveal her innermost being.

A lot of us can't face the thought of people seeing us as we really are— for it means losing control of the public persona we've so carefully maintained. And we never get closer to the truth of our dark, vulnerable, messy selves than with sex. Perhaps that's why the prospect of being unmasked as the author of this book was so very difficult to bear. Perhaps if I was alone, without family around me whom I deeply care about, it would have been easier.

....

At one point she reads a magazine called The Face, *where she comes across references to californication, chili-dogging, daisy-chaining and hum jobs. Then she is "Repelled. Horrified. Wet." Why do you think we might be aroused by sexual practices we'd also call repellent and horrific?*

NIKKI GEMMELL: If we dive deep into the underbelly of anyone's sexuality it is without limitations and standards. As Goethe said, "Baseness attracts everybody." But usually this world is completely hidden: we never know another person's secret life. The most shocking thing about *Bride* is its honesty—and it is the thing that readers respond to the most. So many women have said things like, "This is me. These are my thoughts," or ▶

9

Behind the Scenes (*continued*)

◄ "It struck such a raw nerve with me." Responses like that have made me realize that the book was worth doing.

....

Did you make the bride's first lover, Gabriel, a virgin to reverse the old social stereotype of the male sexually preying upon the virgin female?

NIKKI GEMMELL: I loved the idea of a man who was totally malleable, who would do exactly what a woman wanted, without any preconceived notions of what makes for glorious sex. The most obvious example to use would have been a much younger man, but I didn't want to stray into Mrs. Robinson territory. I wanted something a little more unusual.

....

Catherine Millet, in her memoir, The Sexual Life of Catherine M, *says "Fucking is an antidote to boredom." At times, the bride seems to think the same thing, albeit in less direct language. Would she agree with Millet on this, or is she too drawn to the occasional "charge" in her marriage, and to a relationship that works "enough"?*

NIKKI GEMMELL: Fucking is not an antidote to boredom for my protagonist. She is pushed into illicit sex through extreme pressures. Those pressures are not only a suspected betrayal by her husband but also by a sense that she is becoming subsumed by the role of "wife"; she has lost any sense of her former self. It is a way of reclaiming something of herself, for herself. There is a moral core to *Bride*. My protagonist respects the sanctity of monogamy and is deeply disturbed by the events that unfold in the book. And it's hard to explain, but another reason for the anonymity was that it came from a deep love, a deep sense of compassion. It is the love between a husband and wife that I was most interested in, with all the compromises inherent within that particular relationship, all the mess. Nothing is clean, nothing straightforward, but there can be a tenacious love nonetheless.

....

I've shown a female friend the part of your novel that lists "What you do not want" and "What you want." She checked many of the practices that you listed in the first category, like "A tongue in your ear," "To be asked what are you thinking" and "Any expression like 'Ooh yes, baby' and 'C'mon.'" This

*made me wonder if many men—and not just the bride's husband, Cole—
have it all wrong. Do we?*

Nikki Gemmell: I can't speak for all men, but it's a section of the book
that struck a chord with many women. For this chapter, I emailed about
fifteen girlfriends and asked them to give me just one line on something
they loved a man to do to them during sex, and one thing they couldn't
stand. Most responded, extremely candidly—much more so than in con-
versations we'd ever had. About a third said they didn't like anything to do
with the breasts. Hallelujah! So it wasn't just me—and for a long time I'd
thought I must be frigid in this particular area. And yet this is something
men assume is a key erogenous zone for all women and always make a
beeline for. Where do these sexual myths come from, and why do women
so willingly perpetuate them?

One woman said she couldn't stand a big penis. Right on, girlfriend, I
thought—I really don't like feeling I'm being split apart either. Some
commented on the sounds men made as they were coming. One woman
had a particular hatred of expressions like "Ooh yes, baby," another said
she couldn't stand it when an ex-lover sounded like he was straining on
the toilet. This chapter in particular was meant to be a cheeky kind of
instruction manual for men. The book, after all, is dedicated "To my
husband. To all husbands."

I loved the idea of male readers being sparked by the erotic implications
of a book "By Anonymous" and then actually learning something as they
delved into it. It's not meant to be a comfortable read but a challenging one.
And what is it that men can't stand a woman doing to them while they're
making love? Ah, it's up to someone else to write *The Groom Stripped Bare*. It
could only be a man, and it would have to be written anonymously—for it's
the only way to be rigorously honest. The male writer who's come closest to
that shocking, reckless, exhilarating level of candor is Michel Houellebecq.

....

Yet Houellebecq, whose name has come up in discussions of Bride, *writes
about sexuality in a very clinical manner. Your novel is far less melancholic,
or at any rate it does not push out a heavy message of sociological seriousness,
like his. It wouldn't really fit into the movement that's been called, in part
because of Houellebecq, "depressionism," would it?*

Nikki Gemmell: Goodness, no. I wouldn't include *Bride* in the depressionism movement in any way. My novel is all heart. ▶

Behind the Scenes (*continued*)

....

So who are your literary influences, then? One reviewer compared you to the American novelist Chuck Palahniuk, author of Fight Club. *Is that a fair comparison?*

Nikki Gemmell: Haven't read him, sorry. I'd say *Bride* was more in the vein of extremely raw, unflinching female confessionals like Elizabeth Smart's *By Grand Central Station I Sat Down and Wept.* Actually, the book I was thinking of when I began to write was Alessandro Baricco's *Silk.* I dreamt of something extremely short, elegant and spare. But my books never end up the way I initially envisage them, no matter how much I try to corral them during the writing process. They always assume a life of their own, as *Bride* did very much as I was working on it. She just slipped away from me.

....

Your protagonist—a writer like you—assigns a pivotal role to the ability of words to arouse. Whether it's "the intoxicating smell of paper and leather, of words, waiting" at the library, or "saying all the words that've never slipped comfortably from your tongue: cunt, fuck, ass," there is a quivering eroticism in her experience with words. Why are they so important in a story like this?

Nikki Gemmell: I wanted the reading of the book to be a sensual experience. I wanted there to be a beauty to the words and the honesty; a beauty to the cover, the text, even the paper (of course, publishers aren't quite so keen on the expense of this). But in a way I wanted the reader to be lulled into a false sense of security by the beauty and the sensuality of the whole package—and then be jarred by some extremely raw truths. I love the element of surprise in writing.

....

Why the second-person narrative? A critic in The Independent *wrote that this narrative voice turns your protagonist into an object and, at the same time, forces the reader into the frame. Why did you use this narrative point of view?*

Nikki Gemmell: I was fascinated by that particular tense and wanted to give it a go. It's extremely difficult to sustain—the only book I'd read where it was successfully pulled off was Jay McInerney's *Bright Lights, Big City.* I loved the way the second-person tense implies intimacy and yet also distance. The protagonist is recording events as he witnesses them, but also commenting upon them objectively. Some people have said of my unnamed bride that it was like "reading her brain, being in her head-space," which was exactly the effect I was aiming for—hopefully without too much indulgence.

....

The term "post-feminist" has come up in reviews of Bride. *Is this a post-feminist book in its vindication of marriage and family?*

NIKKI GEMMELL: I was fascinated by the shortcomings of feminism. I consider myself a feminist and yet I still hanker, deeply, for the age-old stereotypes of mother, wife, nester—and that puts me in an odd position. I think a lot of the so-called unfashionable urges that *Bride* explores are deeply biological within many women, and feminism doesn't give them much credit. Nothing is black and white; we're all animals underneath and we have to listen to our bodies. Women, particularly older feminists, have to be more embracing of the choices some younger women are making. We just have to value one another.

Peter Babiak's interview with Nikki Gemmell first appeared in SubTerrain *magazine. He is the Academic Director of Humanities 101 at the University of British Columbia and teaches English literature at Langara College in Vancouver.*

Have You Read?

Nikki Gemmell has published three previous novels.

SHIVER

A young woman, Fin, fulfils her ambition to visit Antarctica, the last great wilderness on earth. Here she integrates with the local community, learning to respect their customs and way of life. But she breaks the strictest taboo of all when she falls in love.

"Her inimitable, urgent and demanding style makes her books impossible to put down or forget."

Madame Figaro

"Gemmell writes brilliantly."

The Sunday Times

ALICE SPRINGS

Snip Freeman lost her father long ago. Accompanied by her new lover, Dave, she embarks on a journey into the vast and fierce landscape of the Australian interior, to find her father and unravel the terrifying silence of her childhood.

"*Alice Springs* is like a female version of Kerouac's *On the Road*."

Cosmopolitan

"Leaks deep into the imagination . . . haunts one long after the book ends."

The Times

LOVESONG

The heartbreaking story of Lillie Bird, a woman from a locked religious community who one day finds herself in the freedom of a strange new world, England, yet accused of murdering a man.

"Gemmell evokes place superbly . . . while Lillie, clever, confused and vulnerable, is real and touching."

The Sunday Times

"A lovely, lyrical creation that has melody and melancholy aching through its sentences . . . bewitchingly good."

Elle, Book of the Month

If you loved this, you'll like . . .

FICTION

Delta of Venus
Anaïs Nin

Lady Chatterley's Lover
D. H. Lawrence

The Hours
Michael Cunningham

The Bell Jar
Sylvia Plath

NONFICTION

The Sexual Life of Catherine M
Catherine Millet

The Feminine Mystique
Betty Friedan

My Secret Garden
Nancy Friday

The Whole Woman
Germaine Greer

FILMS

Betty Blue *(1986)*

Thelma and Louise *(1991)*

Eyes Wide Shut *(1999)*

Y Tu Mamá También *(2001)*

Find Out **More**

Nikki's own website:
www.nikkigemmell.com

An article Nikki wrote for *The Guardian*,
10 July 2003:
**www.guardian.co.uk/women/story/
0,3604,994962,00.html**

An interview with her on Australian television:
**www.abc.net.au/enoughrope/stories/
s912735.htm**

To find out more about Marcel Duchamp's
artwork of the same name:
**www.tate.org.uk/modern/exhibitions/
surrealism/room1.htm**

Share your experiences on the website for
women:
http://www.ivillage.co.uk

Inspired to experiment? Pick out some toys:
www.myla.com

Nikki Gemmell can be contacted through her
publisher:

Perennial
10 East 53rd Street
New York, NY 10022

Don't miss the next book by your favorite author. Sign up now for AuthorTracker by visting www.AuthorTracker.com.